The Greatest Christian Stories Ever Written

The Greatest Christian Stories Ever Written.

Published by Scroll Publishing Company, P. O. Box 122, Amberson, PA 17210. (717) 349-7033. www.scrollpublishing.com.

Write for a free catalog of our publications.

ISBN: 978-0-924722-22-6

Cover art: John Everett Millais

Printed in the United States of America

Contents

Introduction

The stories included in this collection were handpicked for their Christian message. Many of these stories were written by some of the most respected authors of all time. We feel certain that after reading these stories you, too, will agree that these are among the greatest Christian stories ever written.

The stories were selected on the basis of their *message*, not on the worthiness of the authors who wrote them. The authors range from Jesus Christ, the founder of Christianity, to Mark Twain, who remained a skeptic his whole life. Yet, when you read Twain's *The War Prayer*, you'll understand why we chose to include it in this collection. You'll also realize why Twain was skeptical about organized religion. It is tragic that he never met any genuine people of the Kingdom.

Leo Tolstoy wrote several of the stories in this collection. Few persons have embraced Jesus' teachings from the Sermon on the Mount as thoroughly and radically as did Tolstoy. Yet, for most of his life, he struggled with many of the basic Christian theological doctrines.

One of the included authors, Henry Van Dyke, was an ordained minister and hymn writer. Johanna Spyri was a deeply spiritual Christian with a heart for the poor. So the collection of authors span quite a range. However, all of the stories are spiritual masterpieces that point the reader to Jesus Christ, His teachings, and His Kingdom.

The Other Wise Man

Henry Van Dyke

You know the story of the Three Wise Men of the East, and how they traveled from far away to offer their gifts at the manger in Bethlehem. But have you ever heard the story of the Other Wise Man? He also saw the star when it arose, and he set out to follow it. Yet he did not arrive with his brethren when they reached Bethlehem. And so he missed seeing the young child Jesus.

You have probably never heard of this Other Wise Man, and so I want to tell you about him. I want to tell you about the great desire of this fourth pilgrim, and how his desire was denied. And yet in the denial, his desire was fulfilled. I want to tell you of his many wanderings and of the trials of his soul. I wish to tell you of the long search he undertook and of the strange way in which he found the One whom he sought.

Chapter One

In the days when Augustus Caesar was master of many kings and Herod reigned in Jerusalem, there lived in the city of Ecbatana, among the mountains of Persia, a certain man named Artaban. His house stood close to the outermost walls that encircled the royal treasury. From his roof, he could look over the battlements of crimson, blue and red. He could also see the hill where the summer palace of the Persian emperors glittered like a jewel in a crown.

A beautiful garden surrounded Artaban's house. It was a tangle of flowers and fruit-trees, watered by a dozen streams descending from the nearby mountains. The garden was filled with the music of innumerable birds. But all color was lost in the soft and odorous darkness of this late September night. All sounds were hushed in the deep charm of the night's silence, except for the splashing of the water, like a voice half-sobbing and half-laughing under the shadows. High above the trees a dim glow of light shone through the curtained arches of the upper chamber, where the master of the house was holding a council with his friends.

Artaban stood by the doorway to greet his guests. He was a tall, dark man of about forty years, with brilliant eyes set under his broad brow. There were firm lines graven around his fine, thin lips. He had the brow of a dreamer and the mouth of a leader, a man of sensitive feeling but inflexible will. He was one of those who—in whatever age they may live—are born for inward conflict and a life of quest.

His robe was of pure white wool, thrown over a tunic of silk. A white cap rested on his flowing black hair. It was the dress of one of the men known as Magi.

"Welcome!" he said, in his low, pleasant voice, as one after another entered the room. "Welcome, Adar. Peace be with you, Zeresh and Harbon—and with you my father, Tura. You are all welcome. This house grows bright with the joy of your presence."

There were nine of the men, differing widely in age, but alike in the richness of their dress of many-colored silks. They were also alike in the massive golden collars they wore around their necks, marking them as Persian nobles. The circles of gold resting upon their breasts distinguished them as Magi.

They took their places around a small black brazier at the end of the room, where a tiny flame was burning. Standing beside it and waving a handful of thin tamarisk branches above the fire, Artaban fed the fire with dry sticks of pine and fragrant oils. The men all began to pray to God and sing songs of praise to Him.

To be sure, they didn't fully understand everything about God. However, they knew that there was one true God who had created heaven and earth, and they wanted to serve Him. They saw Him only through a dim light, but that light was about to grow much brighter. That light would eventually shine so brightly that not only these men, but the inhabitants of all of the earth would have the opportunity to know the one true God.

The fire rose with their singing, throbbing as if the flame responded to the music—until it cast a bright illumination through the whole apartment, revealing both its simplicity and its splendor.

The floor was laid with tiles of dark blue, veined with white. Pilasters of twisted silver stood out against the blue walls. Azure silk hung from the round, arched windows above them. The vaulted ceiling was adorned with blue stones, like the body of heaven in its clearness, sown with silver stars. At the eastern end of the room, there were two dark red marble pillars.

The doorway between the pillars, which opened upon the terrace of the roof, was covered with a heavy curtain. The curtain was the color of a ripe pomegranate, embroidered with innumerable golden rays shooting upward from the floor. In effect the room was like a quiet, starry night—all azure and silver—flushed in a hue with the rosy promise of the dawn. It was an expression of the character and spirit of the master—just as the house of a man should be.

Artaban turned to his friends when the singing ended, and he invited them to be seated on the couch at the western end of the room.

Looking around the circle of men, he said, "You have come tonight at my call, as faithful scholars, to renew your worship and rekindle your faith in the God of Purity. We do not worship idols and created things like fire, but the One who is Light and Truth. Is it not so, my father?"

"It is well said, my son," answered the venerable Tura. "The enlightened are never idolaters. They lift the veil of form and go into the sanctuary of truth."

"Hear me, then, my father and my friends," said Artaban, "while I tell you of the new light and truth that have come to me through the most ancient of all signs. We have searched the secrets of nature together, and studied the healing virtues of water and fire and the plants. We have also read the books of prophecy in which the future is dimly foretold in words that are hard to understand.

Finally, we have searched the stars for answers. But is not our knowledge of them still incomplete? For there are many stars that lie beyond our horizon—lights that are known only to the dwellers in the lands far to the south, among the spice trees of Arabia and the gold mines of Ophir."

There was a murmur of assent among the listeners.

"There are many things we still do not understand," Artaban continued, "but I believe that a new sunrise will certainly appear in the appointed time. Do not our own books tell us that this will come to pass and that men will see the brightness of a great light?"

"That is true," said the voice of Tura. "All Magi know the ancient prophecy that the Victorious One shall arise out of the number of the prophets in the west country. Around him shall shine a mighty brightness, and he shall make life everlasting, incorruptible, and immortal. Even the dead shall rise again."

"But that is a deep saying," Harbon said, "and it may be that we shall never understand it. It is better to consider the things that are near at hand and to increase the influence of the Magi in our own country. This is better than to look for one who may be a stranger, and to whom we must resign our power."

The others seemed to approve these words. There was a silent feeling of agreement manifest among them. Their looks responded with that indefinable expression that always follows when a speaker has uttered the thought that has been slumbering in the hearts of his listeners. But Artaban turned to Tura with a glow on his face, and said:

"My father, I have kept this prophecy in the secret place of my soul. Religion without a great hope would be like an altar without a living fire. And now the flame has burned more brightly. By the light of it, I have read other words which also have come from the fountain of Truth, and speak yet more clearly of the rising of the Victorious One in his brightness."

Artaban then drew from the breast of his tunic two small rolls of fine parchment with writing upon them. He unfolded them carefully upon his knee and then said, "In the years that are lost in the past, long before our fathers came into the land of Babylon, there were prophets in Chaldea. Hear the words of one of these ancient prophets: 'There shall come a star out of Jacob, and a scepter shall arise out of Israel.'"

The lips of Harbon drew downward with contempt, as he muttered: "Judah was a captive by the waters of Babylon, and the sons of Jacob were in bondage to *our* kings. The tribes of Israel are scattered through the mountains like lost sheep. Rest assured that neither star nor scepter shall arise from the remnant of the Israelites, who now dwell in Judea under the yoke of Rome."

"And yet," answered Artaban, "it was the Hebrew wise man, Daniel, the mighty searcher of dreams and the counselor of kings, who was the most honored and beloved of our great King Cyrus. Daniel proved himself to be a prophet of sure things and a reader of the thoughts of the Eternal. And these are the words that he wrote (Artaban now read from the second scroll): 'Know, therefore, and understand that from the going forth of the commandment to restore Jerusalem, unto the Anointed One, the Prince, the time shall be seven and threescore and two weeks.'"

"But, my son," said Tura, doubtfully, "these are mystical numbers. Who can interpret them, or who can find the key that shall unlock their meaning?"

Artaban answered: "It has been shown to me and to my three companions among the Magi—Caspar, Melchior, and Balthasar. We have searched the ancient tablets of Chaldea and computed the time. It falls in this year. We have studied the sky, and in the spring of the year we saw two of the greatest planets draw near together in the sign of the Fish, which is the house of the Hebrews. We also saw a new star there, which shone for one night and then vanished. Now again the two great planets are meeting. This night is their conjunction. My three brothers are watching at Borsippa, in Babylonia, and I am watching here.

"If the star shines again, they will wait ten days for me at Borsippa, and then we will set out together for Jerusalem, to see and worship the promised one who shall be born King of Israel. I believe the sign will come. I have already prepared for the journey. In fact, I have sold all my possessions and bought these three jewels—a sapphire, a ruby, and a pearl—to carry them as a tribute to this King. And now I ask you to go with me on this pilgrimage, that we may have joy together in finding the Prince who is worthy to be served."

While he was speaking, Artaban thrust his hand into the innermost fold of his robe and drew out three great gems—one as blue as a piece of the sky, one redder than a ray of sunrise, and one as pure as the peak of a snow-covered mountain at twilight. He then laid them on the outspread scrolls before him.

But his friends looked on with skeptical and alien eyes. A veil of doubt and mistrust came over their faces, like a fog creeping up from the marshes to hide the hills. They glanced at each other with looks of wonder and pity—such as those who have listened to unattainable sayings, the story of a wild vision, or the proposal of an impossible undertaking.

At last Harbon said: "Artaban, this is a vain dream. It comes from looking too much upon the stars and the cherishing of lofty thoughts. It would be wiser to spend the time in gathering money for the new temple at Chala. No king will ever rise from the broken race of Israel. And no end will ever come to the eternal strife between light and darkness. He who looks for it is simply a chaser of shadows. Good night."

And another one said: "Artaban, I have no knowledge of these things, and my office as guardian of the royal treasure binds me here. The quest is not for me. But if you must follow it, blessings on your journey."

And still another said: "In my house there sleeps a new bride. I can neither leave her nor take her with me on this strange journey. This quest is not for me. But may your steps be prospered wherever you go. So, farewell."

And another said: "I am ill and unfit for hardship, but there is a man among my servants whom I will send with you when you go, to bring me word of how you fare."

So, one by one, they left the house of Artaban. But Tura, the oldest and the one who loved him the best, lingered after the others had gone. He spoke in a soft voice, "My son, it may be that the light of truth is in this sign that has appeared in the skies. If so, it will surely lead to the Prince and the mighty Brightness. Or it may be that it is only a shadow of the light—as Harbon has said. If so, he who follows it will have a long pilgrimage and a fruitless search. But it is better to follow even the shadow of the best than to remain content with the worst. And those who would see wonderful things must often be ready to travel alone. I am too old for this journey, but my heart shall be a companion to you in your pilgrimage day and night. Go in peace."

Then Tura went out of the azure chamber with its silver stars, and Artaban was left in solitude. He gathered up the jewels and replaced them inside his robe. For a long time he stood and watched the flame that flickered and sank in the brazier. Then he crossed the hall, lifted the heavy curtain, and passed out between the pillars to the terrace on the roof.

The shiver that runs through the earth before she rouses from her night's sleep had already begun. The cool wind that heralds the daybreak was drawing downward from the lofty snow-traced ravines of Mount Orontes. Birds, half-awakened, crept and chirped among the rustling leaves, and the smell of ripened grapes came in brief wafts from the arbors.

Far over the eastern plain, a white mist stretched forth like a lake. But where the distant peaks of Zagros serrated the western horizon, the sky was clear. The planets, Jupiter and Saturn, rolled together like drops of a brilliant flame about to blend into one.

As Artaban watched them, a steel-blue spark was born out of the darkness beneath, rounding itself with purple splendors to a crimson sphere. It spiraled upward through rays of saffron and orange into a point of white radiance. Tiny and infinitely remote, yet perfect in every part, it pulsated in the enormous canvas of the dawn sky. It was as if the three jewels in Artaban's robe had mingled and been transformed into a living heart of light.

He bowed his head and covered his brow with his hands. "It is the sign," he said. "The King is coming, and I will go to meet him."

Chapter Two

All night long, Vashta, the swiftest of Artaban's horses, had been waiting in her stall, saddled and bridled. She was pawing the ground impatiently and shaking her bit. It were as if she shared the eagerness of her master's purpose, though she knew not its meaning.

Before the birds had fully roused to their strong, high, joyful chant of morning song, before the white mist had begun to lift lazily from the plain, the Other Wise Man was in the saddle, riding swiftly along the westward road that skirted the base of Mount Orontes.

How close, how intimate is the comradeship between a man and his favorite horse on a long journey. It is a silent, comprehensive friendship, a union beyond the need of words. They drink at the same wayside springs and sleep under the same stars. They are conscious together of the subduing spell of nightfall and the quickening joy of daybreak. The master shares his evening meal with his hungry companion. He feels the soft, moist lips caressing the palm of his hand as they close over the morsel of bread.

In the gray dawn, the rider is roused from his sleep by the gentle stir of a warm, sweet breath over his sleeping face. He looks up into the eyes of his faithful fellow-traveler, ready and waiting for the toil of the day. Surely, unless he is an unbeliever, he will thank God for this voiceless sympathy, this silent affection. In his morning prayer, he will embrace a double blessing: "God bless us both, the horse and the rider, and keep our feet from falling and our souls from death!"

Then, through the keen morning air, the swift hoofs beat their tattoo along the road, keeping time to the pulsing of two hearts that are moved with the same eager desire—to conquer space, to devour the distance, to attain the goal of the journey.

Artaban must indeed ride wisely and well if he was to keep the appointed hour with the other Magi. For the route was three hundred miles, and thirty miles was the utmost that he could travel in a day. But he knew Vashta's strength, and he pushed forward without anxiety, making the fixed distance every day—even though he had to travel late into the night and get up in the morning long before sunrise.

He passed along the brown slopes of Mount Orontes, furrowed by the rocky courses of a hundred torrents. He crossed the level plains of the Nisaeans, where the famous herds of horses, feeding in the wide pastures, tossed their heads at Vashta's approach and then galloped away with a thunder of many hoofs. Flocks of wild birds rose suddenly from the swampy meadows, wheeling in great circles with a shining flutter of innumerable wings and shrill cries of surprise.

Artaban traversed the fertile fields of Concabar, where the dust from the threshing floors filled the air with a golden mist, half hiding the huge temple of Astarte with its four hundred pillars.

At Baghistan, among the rich gardens watered by fountains from the rock, he looked up at the mountain thrusting its immense rugged brow out over the road. Carved on the mountain, he saw the figure of King Darius trampling upon his fallen foes, and the proud list of his wars and conquests written high upon the face of the timeless cliff.

On and on the horse and rider traveled: Over many a cold and desolate pass, crawling painfully across the wind-swept shoulders of the hills. Down many a black mountain gorge, where a river roared and raced before them like a savage guide. Across many a smiling vale, with terraces of yellow limestone full of vines and fruit trees. Through oak groves and the dark gates of Zagros, walled in by precipices. Into the ancient city of Chala, where the people of Samaria had been kept in captivity long ago. And out again by the mighty portal that had been cut through the encircling hills.

On and on they continued. Past the entrance of the narrow pass through which the river Gyndes foamed down to meet them—filled from end to end with orchards of peaches and figs. Over the broad rice-fields, where the autumnal vapors spread their silent mists. Following along the course of the river, they traveled under tremulous shadows of poplar and tamarind among the lower hills. And then out upon the flat plain, where the road ran straight as an arrow through the stubble-fields and parched meadows. They went past the capital city, where the Parthian emperors reigned, and the vast metropolis of Seleucia that Alexander the Great had built. They crossed the swirling floods of the Tigris and the many channels of the Euphrates, flowing yellow through the fields of corn.

Artaban pressed onward until he arrived beneath the shattered walls of populous Babylon. It was nightfall of the tenth day. Vashta was almost spent, and Artaban wished he could turn into the city to find rest and refreshment for himself and for her. But he knew that it was three hours' journey more to the place of meeting, and he must reach it by midnight if he would join his waiting comrades. So he did not halt, but rode steadily across the stubble-fields.

A grove of date-palms made an island of green in the pale yellow sea. As she passed into the shadow, Vashta slackened her pace and began to pick her way more carefully. Near the far end of the darkness, she suddenly became even more cautious. She sensed some danger or difficulty. It was not in her heart to fly from it—only to be prepared for it and to meet it wisely, as a good horse should. The grove was dark and silent as a tomb. Not a leaf rustled. Not a bird sang.

Vashta stepped very delicately, carrying her head low. She sighed now and then with apprehension. At last she gave a quick breath of anxiety and dismay and stood stock-still, quivering in every muscle. Before her lay a dark object in the shadow of the last palm tree.

Artaban dismounted. The dim starlight revealed the form of a man lying across the road. His humble dress and the outline of his haggard face showed that he was probably one of the Jews who still dwelt in great numbers around the city. His pallid skin—dry and yellow as parchment—bore the mark of the deadly fever that ravaged the marshlands in autumn. The chill of death was in his sinewy hand. As Artaban released it, the arm fell back inertly upon the man's motionless breast.

Artaban turned away with a thought of pity, leaving the body to that strange burial that the Magi deemed most fitting—the funeral of the desert, from which the kites and vultures rise on dark wings, and the beasts of prey slink furtively away. When they are gone, there is only a heap of white bones on the sand.

But, as he turned, a long, faint, ghostly sigh came from the man's lips. The bony fingers gripped the hem of the Magi's robe and held him fast. Artaban's heart leaped to his throat—not with fear—but with an unspoken resentment at this ill-timed delay.

How could he stay here in the darkness to minister to a dying stranger? How could this unknown fragment of human life lay any claim upon his compassion or his service? If he lingered even for an hour, he would never reach Borsippa at the appointed time. His companions would think he had given up the journey. They would go without him. He would lose his quest.

Yet, if he went on now, the man would surely die. If he stayed, he might be able to save the man's life. Artaban's spirit throbbed and fluttered with the urgency of the crisis. Should he risk losing the great reward of his faith for the sake of a single deed of charity? Should he turn aside—if only for a moment—from following the star, to give a cup of cold water to a poor, perishing Jew?

"God of truth and purity," he prayed, "direct me in the holy path, the way of wisdom which only You know."

Then he turned back to the sick man. Loosening the grasp of his hand, he carried him to a little mound at the foot of the palm tree.

Artaban unbound the thick folds of the dying man's turban and opened the garment above his sunken breast. He brought water from one of the small canals nearby, and he moistened the sufferer's brow and mouth. He mingled a cup of one of those simple but potent remedies that he always carried in his robe. For the Magi were physicians as well as star-gazers. He slowly poured the drink between the man's colorless lips. Hour after hour he labored as only a skillful healer of disease can do. At last the man's strength returned. He sat up and looked about him.

"Who are you?" he asked, in the rustic dialect of the country, "and why have you sought me here to bring back my life?"

"I am Artaban, one of the Magi, of the city of Ecbatana. And I am going to Jerusalem in search of one who is to be born King of the Jews, a great Prince and Deliverer of all men. I dare not delay my journey any longer, for the caravan that has waited for me may depart without me. But look, here is all that I have left of bread and water, and here is a potion of healing herbs. They are yours. When your strength is restored, you can find the dwellings of the Jews among the houses of Babylon."

The Jew raised his trembling hand solemnly to heaven and said, "Now may the God of Abraham and Isaac and Jacob bless and prosper the journey of the merciful, and bring him in peace to his desired haven."

Turning to Artaban, the healed man whispered, "I have nothing to give you in return—only this: that I can tell you where the Messiah must be sought. For our prophets have said that he should be born not in Jerusalem, but in Bethlehem of Judah. May the Lord bring you in safety to that place, because you have had pity upon the sick."

It was already long past midnight. Artaban rode in haste, and Vashta, restored by the brief rest, ran eagerly through the silent plain and swam the channels of the river. She exerted the last bit of her strength and fled over the ground like a gazelle.

But the first beam of the rising sun was already casting shadows as she entered upon the final mile of the journey. The eyes of Artaban anxiously scanned the great mound and its ruins—which was their rendezvous point—but he could discern no trace of his friends.

The many-colored terraces of black, orange, red, yellow and green—shattered by the convulsions of nature and crumbling under the repeated blows of human violence—still glittered like a ruined rainbow in the morning light.

Artaban rode swiftly around the hill. He dismounted and climbed to the highest terrace, looking out toward the west. The huge desolation of the marshes stretched away to the horizon and the border of the desert. Bitterns stood by the stagnant pools, and jackals skulked through the low bushes. But there was no sign of the caravan of the Wise Men, neither far nor near.

At the edge of the terrace, Artaban saw a little pile of broken bricks, and under them a piece of papyrus. He picked it up and read: "We have waited past midnight, and can delay no longer. We go to find the King. Follow us across the desert."

Artaban sat down upon the ground and covered his head in despair.

"How can I cross the desert," he said aloud, "with no food and with a spent horse? I must return to Babylon, sell my sapphire, and buy a train of camels and provisions for the journey. I may never catch up with my friends. Only God the merciful knows whether I will miss seeing the King because I tarried to show mercy."

Chapter 3

Weeks passed. But soon the figure of the Other Wise Man could be seen again, passing over the dreary undulations of the desert, high upon the back of his camel, rocking steadily onward like a ship over the waves.

The land of death spread its cruel net around him. The stony waste bore no fruit except briers and thorns. The dark ledges of rock thrust themselves above the surface here and there, like the bones of perished monsters. Arid and inhospitable mountain ranges rose before him, furrowed with dry channels of ancient torrents—white and ghastly, like scars on the face of nature. Shifting hills of treacherous sand were heaped like tombs along the horizon.

By day, the fierce heat pressed its intolerable burden on the quivering air. No living creature moved on the silent, swooning earth—except for tiny jerboas scuttling through the parched bushes or lizards vanishing in the clefts of the rocks. By night the jackals hunted and howled in the distance. The lion made the black ravines echo with his hollow roaring, while a bitter, blighting chill followed the fever of the day. Through heat and cold, Artaban moved steadily onward.

Eventually, Artaban reached the gardens and orchards of Damascus, watered by the streams of Abana and Pharpar. The sloping banks were inlaid with blooms and thickets of myrrh and roses. Artaban saw the long, snowy ridge of Mount Hermon and the dark groves of cedars. He passed the valley of the Jordan, the blue waters of the Sea of Galilee, and the fertile plain of Esdraelon. He rode through the hills of Ephraim and the highlands of Judah—moving steadily onward until he arrived at Bethlehem. But it was now the third day after his friends, the three Wise Men, had come to that place. They had found Mary and Joseph with the young child Jesus, and they had laid their gifts of gold and frankincense and myrrh at his feet.

Now the Other Wise Man drew near. He was weary but full of hope. He still had his ruby and costly pearl to offer to the King. "Now at last," he said, "I shall surely find him—even though I am alone and come to him later than my brethren have. This is the place of which the Jewish exile told me that the prophets had spoken, and here I shall behold the rising of the great Light. But I must inquire about the visit of my brethren, and to what house the star directed them, and to whom they presented their tribute."

The streets of the village seemed to be deserted, and Artaban wondered whether the men had all gone up to the pastures in the hills to bring down their sheep. Through the open door of a cottage, he heard the sound of a woman's voice singing softly. He entered and found a young mother hushing her baby to rest. She told him of the strangers from the far East who had appeared in the village three days before. They said that a star had guided them to the place where Joseph of Nazareth was lodging with his wife and her newborn child. She also told Artaban how these men from the East had paid reverence to the child and given him many precious gifts.

"But the travelers disappeared again," she continued, "as suddenly as they had come. We were afraid at the strangeness of their visit. We could not understand it. The man of Nazareth took the child and his mother, and they fled away that same night secretly. It was whispered that they were going to Egypt. Ever since, there has been an uneasiness among the villagers. Something evil seems to hang over the town. They say that the Roman soldiers are coming from Jerusalem to exact a new tax from us. For that reason, the men have driven the flocks and herds far back among the hills and have hidden themselves."

Artaban listened to her gentle, timid speech. The child in her arms looked up in his face and smiled. He stretched out his rosy hands to grasp at the circle of gold on Artaban's breast. Artaban's heart warmed to the touch. It seemed like a greeting of love and trust to one who had journeyed for a long time in loneliness and perplexity—fighting with his own doubts and fears—and following a light that was veiled in clouds.

"Why could not this child have been the promised Prince?" he asked himself, as he touched the child's soft cheek. "Kings have been born in lowlier houses than this, and the favorite of the stars may rise even from a cottage. But it has not seemed good to the God of wisdom to reward my search so soon and so easily. The One whom I seek has gone before me. And now I must follow this new King to Egypt."

The young mother laid the baby in its cradle, and then she rose to minister to the needs of the strange guest that had come to her house. She set food before him. It was the simple fare of peasants, but willingly offered. Therefore, it was full of refreshment for the soul as well as for the body. Artaban accepted it gratefully. As he ate, the child fell into a happy slumber, and murmured sweetly in his dreams. A great peace filled the room.

But suddenly there came the noise of a wild confusion in the streets of the village: the shrieking and wailing of women's voices, the sound of brazen trumpets, and the clash of swords. And then a desperate cry rang out: "The soldiers! The soldiers of Herod! They're killing our children."

The young mother's face grew white with terror. She clasped her child to her bosom, and crouched motionless in the darkest corner of the room, covering him with the folds of her robe, lest he should awake and cry.

But Artaban went quickly and stood in the doorway of the house. His broad shoulders filled the portal from side to side, and the top of his cap nearly touched the lintel.

The soldiers came hurrying down the street with bloody hands and dripping swords. At the sight of the stranger in his imposing dress, they hesitated with surprise. The captain of the band approached the door to thrust him aside. But Artaban did not move. His face was as calm as though he were watching the stars. In his eyes there burned that steady radiance before which even the half-tamed hunting leopard shrinks and the bloodhound pauses in its leap. He held the soldier silently for an instant, and then said in a quiet voice:

"I am all alone in this place, and I am waiting to give this jewel to the prudent captain who will leave me in peace."

He showed the ruby, glistening in the hollow of his hand like a great drop of blood.

The captain was amazed at the splendor of the gem. The pupils of his eyes expanded with desire, and the hard lines of greed wrinkled around his lips. He stretched out his hand and took the ruby.

"March on!" he cried to his men, "there is no child here. The house is empty."

The clamor and the clang of arms passed down the street just like the headlong fury of chasing hounds sweeps by the secret covert where the trembling deer is hidden. Artaban re-entered the cottage. He turned his face to heaven and prayed:

"God of truth, forgive my sin! I have said something that is not true, to save the life of a child. And two of my gifts are gone. I have spent for man that which was meant for God. Shall I ever be worthy to see the face of the King?"

But the voice of the woman, weeping for joy in the shadow behind him, said very gently: "Because you have saved the life of my little one, may the Lord bless you and keep you. The Lord make His face to shine upon you and be gracious unto you. The Lord lift up His countenance upon you and give you peace."

Chapter 4

The years passed as Artaban continued his quest. He could be seen moving among the throngs of men in crowded Egypt, seeking everywhere for traces of the household that had come down from Bethlehem. Artaban could be seen under the spreading sycamore trees of Heliopolis, and beneath the walls of the Roman fortress beside the Nile. But traces of the family from Bethlehem were so faint and dim that they vanished before him continually—like footprints on the wet river sand that glisten for a moment with moisture and then disappear.

He was seen again at the foot of the pyramids, which lifted their sharp points into the intense saffron glow of the sunset sky. The pyramids stood as changeless monuments to the perishable glory of man. Artaban looked up into the face of the crouching Sphinx and vainly tried to read the meaning of the calm eyes and smiling mouth. Was his smile mocking all effort and all aspiration, as had Harbon? Was his smile saying that Artaban's life was all a cruel riddle that has no answer? Was he on a search that never can succeed? Or was there a touch of pity and encouragement in that inscrutable smile? Was there a promise that even the defeated can attain victory and the disappointed can discover the prize they seek? Was there a promise that the ignorant can be made wise, that the blind will see, and the wanderer will reach his haven at last?

Artaban searched for the family from Bethlehem throughout all of Egypt, but he never found them.

Years later he was seen in an obscure house in Alexandria, taking counsel with a Jewish rabbi. The venerable man, bending over the rolls of parchment on which the prophecies of Israel were written, read aloud the sad words that foretold the sufferings of the promised Messiah—the despised and rejected of men, the man of sorrows, the one acquainted with grief.

"And remember, my son," the rabbi said, fixing his eyes upon Artaban's face, "the King whom you seek is not to be found in a palace, nor among the rich and powerful. If the light of the world and the glory of Israel had been appointed to come with the greatness of earthly splendor, it would have appeared long ago. For no son of Abraham will ever again rival the power that Joseph had in the palaces of Egypt, or the magnificence of Solomon enthroned between the lions in Jerusalem. But the light for which the world is waiting is a new light, the glory that shall rise out of patient and triumphant suffering. And the kingdom that is to be established forever is a new kingdom, the royalty of unconquerable love.

"I do not know how this shall come to pass," the rabbi continued, "nor how the turbulent kings and peoples of earth shall be brought to acknowledge the Messiah and pay homage to him. But this I know: Those who seek him will do well to look among the poor and the lowly, the sorrowful and the oppressed."

So the Other Wise Man continued his journey, traveling from place to place, and searching among the Jews of the Dispersion, with whom the little family from Bethlehem might, perhaps, have found a refuge. He passed through countries where famine lay heavy upon the land, and the poor were crying for bread. He made his dwelling in plague-stricken cities, where the sick were languishing in the bitter companionship of helpless misery.

He visited the oppressed and the afflicted in the gloom of subterranean prisons, and the crowded wretchedness of slave markets, and the weary toil of galley ships. In all this populous and intricate world of anguish, he did not find the One whom he sought to worship. But he found many whom he could help. He fed the hungry, clothed the naked, healed the sick, and comforted the captive.

His years passed more swiftly than a weaver's shuttle that flashes back and forth through the loom while the cloth grows and the pattern is completed. It seemed almost as if he had forgotten his quest.

One morning he stood alone at sunrise, resting on the banks of a gently flowing river. He took the last of his jewels—the pearl—from its hiding place deep within his robe. As he carefully examined it, a mellower luster—a soft and iridescent light, full of shifting gleams of azure and rose—danced upon its surface. The pearl seemed to have absorbed some reflection of the sapphire and ruby that had already been spent. Like the pearl, the deep purpose of a noble life draws into itself the memories of past joy and past sorrow. All that has helped it, and all that has hindered it, is transfused by a subtle wonder into its very essence. One's life pursuit becomes more luminous and precious the longer it is carried close to the warmth of the beating heart.

Chapter 5

Thirty-three years of Artaban's life had now been spent on his great quest. Yet, he was still a pilgrim and a seeker after the true Light. His hair, once darker than the cliffs of Zagros, was now as white as the wintry snow that covered them. His eyes, which once flashed like flames of fire, were now as dull as embers smoldering among the ashes.

Worn, weary and ready to die—but still looking for the King—he had come for the last time to Jerusalem. Through the years, he had often visited the holy city. He had searched all its lanes, its crowded hovels and black prisons without finding any trace of the family of Nazarenes who had fled from Bethlehem long ago. But now he was determined to make one last effort. And something whispered in his heart that, at last, he might succeed.

It was the season of the Passover. The city was thronged with strangers. The people of Israel, scattered in faraway lands, had returned to the Temple for the great feast. There had been a confusion of tongues in the narrow streets for many days.

But on this day a singular agitation was visible in the multitude. The sky was veiled with a portentous gloom. Currents of excitement seemed to flash through the crowd. A secret tide was sweeping them all one way. The clatter of sandals—and the soft, thick sound of thousands of bare feet shuffling over the stones—flowed unceasingly along the street that leads to the Damascus gate of Jerusalem.

Artaban joined a group of people from his own country, Parthian Jews who had come up to keep the Passover. He asked them what was the cause of the tumult and where they were going.

"We are going," they answered, "to the place called Golgotha, outside the city walls, where there is to be an execution. Have you not heard what has happened? Two famous robbers are to be crucified, and with them another, called Jesus of Nazareth, a man who has done many wonderful works among the people, so that they love him greatly. But the priests and elders have said that he must die, because he claimed to be the Son of God. And Pilate has ordered him to be crucified because he said that he was the King of the Jews."

How strangely these familiar words fell upon the tired heart of Artaban! They had led him for a lifetime over land and sea. And now they came to him mysteriously, like a message of despair. The King had come, but he had been denied and cast out. He was about to perish. Perhaps he was already dying. Could he be the same one who had been born in Bethlehem thirty-three years before, at whose birth the star had appeared in heaven? Could he be the One whose coming the prophets had foretold?

Artaban's heart beat unsteadily with troubled, doubtful apprehension. But he said to himself: "The ways of God are stranger than men can imagine, and it may be that I shall find the King, at last, in the hands of his enemies. Perhaps I shall come in time to offer my pearl for his ransom before they kill him."

So the old man followed the multitude with slow and painful steps toward the Damascus gate of the city. Just beyond the entrance of the guardhouse, a troop of Macedonian soldiers came down the street, dragging a young girl with torn dress and disheveled hair. As Artaban paused to look at her with compassion, she broke suddenly from the hands of her tormentors, and threw herself at his feet, clasping him around the knees. She had seen his clothing and recognized him to be one of the Magi.

"Have pity on me," she cried, "and save me, for the sake of the God of Purity! I also am a daughter of the religion that is taught by the Magi. My father was a merchant of Parthia, but he is dead. And now I have been seized for his debts to be sold as a slave. Save me from this fate worse than death!"

Artaban trembled. It was the old conflict in his soul, which had first come to him in the palm grove of Babylon and then at the cottage in Bethlehem. It was the conflict between the expectation of faith and the impulse of love. Twice before the gifts that he had consecrated to the worship of *God* had been used in the service of *humanity*. This was the third trial, the ultimate test, the final and irrevocable choice.

Was it his great opportunity, or his last temptation? He could not tell. But it was clear in the darkness of his mind that it was inevitable. And does not the inevitable come from God? And in his divided heart, he felt one thing to be certain—to rescue this helpless girl would be a true deed of love. And is not love the light of the soul?

So he slowly took the pearl from inside his robe. Never had it seemed so luminous, so radiant, so full of tender, living luster. He laid it in the hand of the slave girl.

"This is your ransom, daughter! It is the last of my treasures that I was saving for the King."

While he spoke, the darkness of the sky grew deeper, and shuddering tremors ran through the earth. The ground heaved convulsively like the breast of one who struggles with mighty grief.

The walls of the houses rocked to and fro. Stones were loosened and crashed into the street. Dust clouds filled the air. The soldiers fled in terror, reeling like drunken men. But Artaban and the girl whom he had ransomed crouched helplessly beneath the wall of the Praetorium.

What had he to fear? What had he to hope? He had given away the last remnant of his tribute for the King. He had parted with the last hope of finding him. The quest was over, and it had failed. But, even in that thought—accepted and embraced—there was peace. It was neither resignation nor submission. It was something more profound and searching. He knew that all was well, because he had done the best that he could from day to day. He had been true to the light that had been given to him.

He had looked for more. And if he had not found it, if failure was all that came out of his life, doubtless that was the best that was possible. He had not seen the revelation of "life everlasting, incorruptible and immortal." But he knew that even if he could live his earthly life over again, it could not be otherwise than it had been.

One more lingering pulsation of the earthquake quivered through the ground. A heavy tile, shaken from the roof, fell and struck the old man on his temple. He lay gasping for breath and pale, with his gray head resting on the young girl's shoulder. Blood trickled from his wound. As the girl bent over him, fearing that he was dead, there came a voice through the twilight. It was very small and still, like music sounding from a distance, in which the notes are clear but the words are lost. The girl turned to see if someone had spoken from the window above them, but she saw no one.

Then the old man's lips began to move, as if in answer, and she heard him say in the Persian tongue:

"Not so, my Lord! For when did I see you hungry and feed you? Or thirsty, and give you drink? When did I see you a stranger and take you in? Or naked, and clothed you? When did I see you sick or in prison, and come to you? Thirty-three years have I looked for you. Yet, I have never seen your face, nor ministered to you, my King."

He ceased speaking, and the sweet voice came again. And again the girl heard it, very faint and far away. But now she understood the words:

"Truly I say unto you, inasmuch as you have done it unto one of the least of these my brethren, you have done it unto me."

A calm radiance of wonder and joy lit the pale face of Artaban. It was like the first ray of dawn on a snowy mountain peak. A long breath of relief exhaled gently from his lips.

His journey had ended. His treasures were accepted. The Other Wise Man had found the King.

The Wise Teacher

Traditional

Long ago, in the small village of Kadisha, situated in the mountains of Lebanon, there lived a wise teacher. One day three of the children from the village walked to the small hut where the teacher lived, at the edge of the village. The teacher was an old man with white hair and a large white beard that cascaded down his chest. He loved children and was delighted to have these three young visitors come to his house.

"What are your names, my dear children," the old teacher asked.

"My name is Nairi," one of the girls answered immediately. "And I will be ten next week."

"I'm Adar," a dark-haired boy answered next. "And I'm eight."

"And what about you?" the teacher asked, looking at the third child, a young, olive-skinned girl.

"I'm Eanna," the girl replied, "and I'm almost eight."

"Well come inside my house," the teacher said. He served the children honey cakes and goat's milk, and asked them more questions about themselves. He then said, "Now I have a game I want to play with you. Children, do you see that large water jar outside?"

"Yes, teacher, we do," the children replied.

"Good. Follow me over to it," the wise teacher directed.

When they all reached the large empty water jar, the teacher then explained how they were going to play the game.

"Nairi, over there by the woods, there is a pile of large rocks. Do you see them?"

"Yes," Nairi quickly volunteered.

"Wonderful. Each of those rocks is about as big as a man's fist. Now, I want you to go over there and bring back enough of those fist-sized rocks to fill this empty jar." Nairi set off at once to fetch the rocks.

As Nairi was busy with her task, the teacher turned to Eanna. "Now, Eanna," the teacher said, "I want you to go inside my house. In the front room, you'll see a chest. Open the chest, and bring me the linen sack that is inside it. It's full of small glass marbles." Eanna immediately scampered to the door of the teacher's house.

Finally, the teacher turned his attention to Adar. He picked up a bucket and shovel that were on his porch and handed them to Adar. "Adar," the teacher said, "I want you to go behind my house. There you'll see a large pile of sand. I want you to bring back enough bucketfuls of sand to fill this jar."

The teacher rested in the cool shade of his porch while the children completed their tasks. When they had finished, they showed the teacher what they had accomplished. Nairi stood by her pile of large rocks. Next to her, Eanna was sitting on the ground with the sack full of marbles at her feet. Adar, too, was resting on the ground, next to the pile of sand he had brought.

"How do we play this game?" the children now queried.

"We're going to fill the jar," the teacher replied, as he carried the heavy jar off the porch and placed it in front of the children. He paused for a few minutes to catch his breath, and then he continued, "Adar, I want you to keep shoveling sand into the jar until it is full to the brim. Adar responded with enthusiasm. He soon filled the jar with sand.

"That's very good, Adar," the teacher said. "Now, I want you Eanna to take your marbles and add them to the jar—and then I'll have Nairi add her rocks."

Eanna approached the jar skeptically with her sack of marbles. She tried pouring them into the jar, but the jar was so full of sand that they just rolled off the top of the sand onto the ground. "I can't do it," Eanna protested. "The jar is already full."

"You're quite right," the teacher agreed. "There's no room for your marbles, let alone Nairi's rocks. So maybe we had better start over. If the three of you will help me, let's turn the jar over and empty the sand out."

The three children eagerly helped the old teacher turn the jar over, and with the assistance of the shovel they were able to remove all of the sand. "Now," said the teacher, "this time let's start with you, Nairi. Take your rocks and fill the jar with them."

Nairi did as she was asked. Before long, she had filled the jar with her large rocks. "Now," the teacher said, "I want you, Eanna, to pour your sack of marbles into the jar."

Eanna walked over to the jar and began pouring her marbles into it. Being small, the marbles fell down between the rocks. When she could fit in no more marbles, she and the teacher shook the jar back and forth, allowing the marbles to settle between the rocks.

They did this several times, and eventually Eanna was able to fit all of her marbles into the jar.

"Now it's your turn, Adar," the teacher said with a twinkle in his eye. "Use your shovel to start filling the jar with your sand."

Adar took a shovelful of sand and poured it into the jar. The grains of sand were able to flow between both the rocks and the marbles. By shaking the jar several times, Adar was able to fit in quite a few shovelfuls of sand before the jar would hold no more.

"Now, I want you to all sit down on the ground," the teacher told the children, "and I'm going to explain to you the meaning of this game."

He explained: "The rocks, marbles, and sand stand for three things in life. The rocks represent your service to God and His kingdom—and to your fellow man. The marbles represent the physical needs of life: food, clothing, shelter, and things like that. The sand represents things that can make life enjoyable, but which are not necessities—things like amusements, fine dinners, and colorful clothes."

"What happened when we put the sand in the jar before the rocks and marbles? There was no room for the rocks and marbles, was there?"

"It's that way in life as well," the teacher continued. If you fill your life with amusements, fine dinners, and things like that, you will find that there is no room for God. You may even struggle to provide for the necessities of life. On the other hand, if you put God and His kingdom first in your life, He will make certain that all of your necessities are taken care of. There will even be room in your life for a moderate amount of amusements and physical pleasures."

How Much Land Does a Man Need?

Leo Tolstoy

There once was a peasant named Josef who worked hard and honestly for his family, but who had no land of his own, so he always remained as poor as the next man. "Busy as we are from childhood tilling the earth," he often thought, "we peasants will always die as we are living, with nothing of our own. If only we had our own land, it would be different."

Now, close to Josef's village there lived a lady, a small landowner, who had an estate of about three hundred acres. One winter the news got around that the lady was going to sell her land. Josef heard that a neighbor of his was buying fifty acres and that the lady had consented to accept one half in cash and to wait a year for the other half.

"Look at that," Josef thought. "The land is being sold, and I shall get none of it." So he spoke to his wife. "Other people are buying it, and we must also buy twenty acres or so. Life is becoming impossible without land of our own."

So they put their heads together and considered how they could manage to buy it. They had one hundred rubles laid by. They sold a colt and one half of their bees. They then hired out one of their sons as a laborer, and took his wages in advance. They borrowed the rest from a brother-in-law. And so they scraped together half of the purchase money. Having done this, Josef chose forty acres of the lady's farmland, some of it wooded, and went to the lady and bought it.

So now Josef had land of his own. He borrowed seed and sowed it, and the harvest was a good one. Within a year, he had managed to pay off his debts to the lady and to his brother-in-law. So he became a landowner, plowing and sowing his own land, making hay on his own land, cutting his own trees, and feeding his cattle on his own pasture. When he went out to plow his fields, or to look at growing corn, or at his meadows, his heart would fill with joy. The grass that grew and the flowers that bloomed there seemed to be unlike any that grew elsewhere. Formerly, when he had passed this land, it had appeared the same as any other land, but now it seemed quite different.

One day Josef was sitting at home when a peasant passing through the village happened to stop in. Josef asked him where he came from, and the stranger answered that he came from around the Volga River, where he had been working. One word led to another, and the man went on to say that much of the land there was for sale and that many people were moving there to buy it. The land was so good, he said, that the rye sown on it grew as high as a horse. It was so thick that five cuts of a sickle made a sheaf. He said that one peasant had brought nothing with him but his bare hands, and now he has six horses and two cows of his own.

Hearing this, Josef's heart was filled with desire. "Why should I suffer in a narrow hole here," he thought, "if one can live so well elsewhere? I could sell my land and my homestead here. With the money, I will be able to make a fresh start over there and get everything new.

So Josef sold his land, homestead and cattle—all at a profit—and he moved his family to the new settlement. Everything the peasant told him was true, and Josef was ten times better off than he been before. He bought plenty of fertile land and pasture, and he could raise as many head of cattle as he liked.

At first, in the bustle of building and settling down, Josef was pleased with everything in his new place. However, when he got used to it, he began to think that even here he was not satisfied. He wanted to sow more wheat, but there was not enough land of his own for the purpose. Therefore, he rented extra land for three years. The seasons turned out well and the crops were good, so that he began to set money aside. He might have gone on living comfortably, but he grew tired of having to rent other people's land every year—and having to scramble to pay for it.

"If it were all my own land," Josef thought, "I would be independent, and there would be none of this unpleasantness."

Then one day a passing land dealer said he was just returning from the land of the Turks far away.

He told Josef that he had bought thirteen thousand acres of land there, all for only one thousand rubles.

"All one has to do is to make friends with the chiefs," he said. "I gave away about one hundred rubles' worth of dressing gowns and carpets, besides a case of tea. In addition, I gave wine to those who would drink it. As a result, I got the land for less than two pennies an acre."

"That's the answer," thought Josef. "Out there I can get more than ten times as much land as I have now. I must try it."

So Josef left his family to look after the homestead and started on the journey, taking his servant with him. They stopped at a town on their way, and bought a case of tea, some wine, and other presents — just as the tradesman had advised him. On and on they went until they had gone more than three hundred miles. Finally, on the seventh day they came to a place where the Turks had pitched their tents.

As soon as they saw Josef, they came out of their tents and gathered around their visitor. They gave him tea and juice, and had a sheep killed. They then gave him mutton to eat. Josef took presents out of his cart and distributed them to his hosts. He then told them he had come to talk about buying some land. The Turks seemed very glad, and told him he must talk to their chief about it. So they sent for the chief and explained to him why Josef had come.

The chief listened for awhile, then he made a sign with his hand for them to be silent. Addressing himself to Josef, he said: "Well, let it be so. Choose whatever piece of land you like. We have plenty of it."

"And what will be the price?" asked Josef.

"Our price is always the same: one thousand rubles a day."

Josef didn't understand. "A day? What measure is that? How many acres would that be?"

" We do not know how to measure it out," said the chief "So we sell it by the day. As much as you can travel around on your feet in a day is yours, and the price is one thousand rubles."

Josef was surprised.

"But in a day you can walk around a large tract of land," he said.

The chief laughed.

"It will all be yours!" he said. "But there is one condition: if you don't return on the same day to the spot from where you started, your money is lost."

"But how am I to mark the circuit that I have traveled?"

"Why, we shall go to any spot you like and stay there. You will then start from that spot and make your round, taking a spade with you. Wherever you think necessary, make a mark. At every turn you make, dig a hole and pile up the turf. Afterward we will go around with a plow from hole to hole. You may make as large a circuit as you please, but before the sun sets you must return to the place you started from. All the land you cover will be yours."

Josef was delighted. It was decided he would start early the next morning. They talked awhile, and after drinking some more juice and eating some more mutton, they had tea again. Finally, the night came on. They gave Josef a featherbed to sleep on, and the Turks dispersed for the night, promising to assemble the next morning at daybreak and ride out before sunrise to the appointed spot.

Josef lay on the featherbed, but could not sleep. He kept thinking about the land. "What a large tract I will mark off!" he thought. "I can easily do thirty-five miles in a day. The days are long now, and within a circuit of thirty-five miles what a lot of land there will be! I will sell the poorer land, or perhaps rent it out to peasants. However, I'll pick out the best for myself and farm it. Not only that, but I'll buy two ox teams, and hire two more laborers. I'll cultivate or plant about a hundred and fifty acres, and I will pasture cattle on the rest.

Looking around, he saw through the open door that the dawn was breaking. "It's time to wake them up," he thought. "We ought to be starting."

So he got up, roused his servant (who was sleeping in his cart), told him to harness the horses, and he went to call the Turks. "It's time to go to the prairie to measure the land," he said.

The Turks arose and met together, and the chief came too. Then they began drinking tea again, and they offered some to Josef. But he didn't want to waste any more time.

"If we're to go, let's go. It is high time," he said.

So the Turks got ready and they all began journeying to the designated spot. Some of them were mounted on horses, and some were in carts. Josef drove in his own small cart with his servant, and he took a spade with him. When they reached the prairie, the morning sky was beginning to turn red. They ascended a hill and—dismounting from their carts and their horses—gathered together in one spot. The chief came up to Josef and stretched out his arm toward the plain.

"See," he said, "all this, as far as your eye can reach, is available. You may have any part of it you like."

"Josef's eyes glistened: it was all virgin land, as flat as the palm of his hand. The soil was as black as the seed of a poppy, and in the hollows different kinds of grasses grew as high as his chest.

The chief took off his fox fur cap, placed it on the ground and said, "This will be the mark. Start from here and return here again. All the land you go around shall be yours."

Josef took out his money and put it on the cap. Then he took off his outer coat, remaining in his sleeveless undercoat. He unfastened his belt and tied it tight below his stomach, put a little bag of bread into the breast of his coat, and tied a water bottle to his belt. He then drew up the tops of his boots, took the spade from his servant, and stood ready to start. He pondered for awhile which way he should go, for it was tempting in every direction.

"Well, it doesn't matter," he concluded, "I'll just go toward the rising sun."

He turned his face to the east, stretched himself, and waited for the sun to appear above the rim.

"I must lose no time," he thought, "and it's easier walking while it's still cool."

The sun's rays had hardly flashed above the horizon, before Josef went down into the prairie, carrying the spade over his shoulder.

Josef started walking neither slowly nor quickly. After having gone a thousand yards he stopped, dug a hole, and placed pieces of turf one on another to make it more visible. Then he moved on. Now that he had walked off his stiffness he quickened his pace. After awhile he dug another hole.

Josef looked back. The hill could be distinctly seen in the sunlight, with the people on it, and the painted cart wheels. At a rough guess, Josef concluded that he had walked three miles. It was growing warmer. So he took off his undercoat, flung it across his shoulder, and went on again. It had grown quite warm now. He looked at the sun; it was time to think of breakfast.

"The first shift is done," he said to himself, "but there are four shifts in a day, and it's too soon to turn quite yet. But I will take off my boots to make the traveling easier."

He sat down, took off his boots, stuck them into his belt, and went on. It was easy walking now.

"I'll go on for another three miles," he thought, "and then turn to the left. This spot is so fine that it would be a pity to lose it. The further I go, the better the land seems to be."

He went straight on for awhile further. When he looked back, the hill was scarcely visible. The people on it looked like black ants, and he could just barely see something glistening there in the sun.

"Ah," thought Josef, "I have gone far enough in this direction, it's time to turn. Besides I'm sweating heavily, and I'm very thirsty."

He stopped, dug a large hole, and heaped up pieces of turf. Next he untied his water bottle, had a drink, and then turned sharply to the left. He plodded on and on. The grass was high, and it was very hot. Josef now began to grow tired. He looked at the sun and saw that it was noon.

"Well," he thought, "I must rest awhile."

He sat down, ate some bread, and drank some water. But he didn't dare lie down, thinking that if he did he might fall asleep. After resting a little while, he went on again. At first he walked easily, for the food had strengthened him. But by now it had become terribly hot, and he felt sleepy. However, he still lumbered on, thinking: "I may suffer for an hour, but I'll have a lifetime to enjoy this land."

He went a long way in this new direction, and was about to turn left again, when he noticed a damp hollow: "It would be a pity to leave that out," he thought. "Flax would do well there." So he went on past the hollow, and dug a hole on the other side of it before he turned the corner. He had walked about twelve miles since the first corner. Josef looked toward the hill. The heat made the air hazy. It seemed to be quivering, and through the haze the people on the hill could scarcely be seen.

"Ah!" thought Josef, "I have made the sides too long. I must make this one shorter." And he went along the third side, stepping faster. He looked at the sun. It was nearly halfway to the horizon, and he had not yet done two miles of the third side of the square. He was still ten miles from the goal.

"No," he thought, "although it will make my land lopsided, I must hurry back in a straight line now. Otherwise, I might not be able to finish. As it is, I have a great deal of land. So Josef hurriedly dug a hole, and turned straight toward the hill.

Josef now walked with difficulty. He was tired from the heat, his bare feet were cut and bruised, and his legs began to fail him. He longed to rest, but it was impossible if he was to get back before sunset. The sun waits for no man, and it was sinking lower and lower.

"Oh dear," he thought, "I hope I haven't blundered by trying to get too much! What if I get back too late?"

He looked toward the hill and then at the sun. He was still far from his goal, and the sun was already near the rim. Josef trudged on and on. It was very hard walking, but he went faster and faster. Although he pressed on, he was still far from the starting place. He threw away his coat, his boots, and his cap—keeping only the spade, which he used as a support. He then began running.

"What shall I do," he thought again. "I have tried to gain too much land and have ruined the whole affair. I can't get back before the sun sets."

And this fear made him still more breathless. Josef went on running, his soaked shirt and trousers stuck to him, and his mouth was parched. His lungs were working like a blacksmith's bellows and his heart was beating like a hammer. His legs were giving way as if they didn't even belong to him. Josef was terrified that he might die of the strain.

Though afraid of death, he couldn't stop. "After having run all that way, they will call me a fool if I stop now," he said to himself. And so he ran on and on. As he drew nearer, he heard the Turks yelling and shouting to him. Their cries enflamed his heart still more. He gathered his last bit of strength and ran on.

The sun was now close to the horizon. Cloaked in mist, it looked large. And it was as red as blood. "Now, yes now, it's going to set!" Josef cried desperately. But then he noticed that even though the sun was quite low, he was also quite near the starting point. In fact, he could already see the people on the hill waving their arms to hurry him up. He could even see the fox fur cap on the ground—and the money on it. The chief was still sitting on the ground next to it.

"There's plenty of land here alright," he thought to himself. "But will God let me live on it? I've lost my life! I've lost my life! I'll never reach that spot!"

Josef looked at the sun, which by now had reached the earth. One side of it had already disappeared. With all his remaining strength, he rushed on, bending his body forward so that his legs could hardly follow fast enough to keep him from falling. Just as he reached the hill, it suddenly grew dark. He looked up and realized that the sun had already set!

He gave a cry of despair: "All my labor has been in vain," he thought. He was about to stop, but he noticed that the Turks were still shouting. He then realized that although the sun seemed to have set on the *plains*, the men on the hill could still see it. He took a long breath, and dashed up the hill. It was still light there. He reached the top and saw the cap. Next to it sat the chief laughing and holding his sides. Josef uttered a cry. His legs gave way beneath him, he fell forward and reached the cap with his hands.

"Ah, that's a clever fellow!" exclaimed the chief. "He has gained much land!"

Josef's servant came running up and tried to raise him, but he saw that blood was flowing from his mouth. Josef was dead!

The Turks clicked their tongues to show their pity.

His servant picked up the spade and dug a grave long enough for Josef to lie in, and buried him in it. Six feet from his head to his heels—that was all he needed.

The Prodigal Son

Jesus Christ

A certain man had two sons. And the younger of them said to his father, "Father, give me the portion of goods that falls to me."

So he divided to them his livelihood. And not many days after, the younger son gathered all together, journeyed to a far country, and there wasted his possessions with prodigal living. But when he had spent all, there arose a severe famine in that land, and he began to be in want. Then he went and joined himself to a citizen of that country, and he sent him into his fields to feed swine. And he would gladly have filled his stomach with the pods that the swine ate, and no one gave him anything.

But when he came to himself, he said, "How many of my father's hired servants have bread enough and some to spare. And yet I perish with hunger! I will arise and go to my father, and will say to him, 'Father, I have sinned against heaven and before you, and I am no longer worthy to be called your son. Make me like one of your hired servants.'"

And he arose and came to his father. But when he was still a great way off, his father saw him and had compassion, and ran and fell on his neck and kissed him. And the son said to him, "Father, I have sinned against heaven and in your sight, and am no longer worthy to be called your son."

But the father said to his servants, "Bring out the best robe and put it on him, and put a ring on his hand and sandals on his feet. And bring the fatted calf here and kill it, and let us eat and be merry. For this my son was dead and is alive again; he was lost and is found." And they began to be merry.

Now his older son was in the field. And as he came and drew near to the house, he heard music and dancing. So he called one of the servants and asked what these things meant. And he said to him, "Your brother has come, and because he has received him safe and sound, your father has killed the fatted calf."

But he was angry and would not go in. Therefore his father came out and pleaded with him. So he answered and said to his father, "Look, these many years I have been serving you. I never transgressed your commandment at any time. And yet you never gave me a young goat, that I might make merry with my friends. But as soon as this son of yours came, who has devoured your livelihood with harlots, you killed the fatted calf for him."

And his father said to him, "Son, you are always with me, and all that I have is yours. It was right that we should make merry and be glad, for your brother was dead and is alive again, and was lost and is found."[1]

---

[1] Luke 15:11-32 (NKJV)

The Silver Mine

Selma Lagerlof

In a small village of Sweden there once lived five men who went on a moose hunt. One of them was the parson; two were brothers, named Eric and Olaf; the fourth man was the innkeeper; and the fifth was a peasant named Israel.

These men were good hunters who usually were successful on their hunts. However, that day they wandered long and far without getting anything. They grew very discouraged and finally sat down to talk about what they should do. Suddenly the parson saw something that glittered where he had kicked away a tuft of moss. He picked up a sliver of stone that was embedded in the moss, and he noticed how it shone.

"Is it possible that this stuff is lead?" he asked.

Then the others sprang up and scraped away the turf with the butt end of their rifles. When they did this, they saw plainly that a broad vein of ore ran through the mountain.

"What do you think this might be?" asked the parson.

The men chipped off pieces of stone and bit into them. "It must be lead—or at least zinc," they said.

"And the whole mountain is full of it!" chimed in the innkeeper excitedly.

The parson and his companions were very happy. They realized that now they had found great wealth.

"I'll never have to do any more work," one man said.

Another said, "Now I can afford to do nothing at all the whole week through. And on Sundays, I'll drive to church in a golden carriage!"

The men put back the tuft of moss to conceal the vein of ore. Then they carefully noted where the place was. On the way home, they agreed that the parson should travel to Tranhult to ask the mining expert what kind of ore this was. He was to return as soon as possible. Until then, they promised one another not to reveal to a single soul where the ore had been found.

Having made this agreement, the parson departed with a few samples of ore in his pockets. He was just as happy at the thought of being rich as the others were. He envisioned how he would rebuild the parsonage and have a comfortable living. After riding two days, he reached Tranhult and showed his bits of ore to the expert there.

"No, it's not lead," the mineralogist said.

"Perhaps it's zinc, then," said the parson.

"No, it's not zinc, either."

The parson thought that all was lost, and the hope within him sank. He hadn't been so depressed in many a long day.

"Have you many stones like this in your parish?" asked the mineralogist.

"We have a whole mountain full," the parson replied.

Hearing that, the mineralogist came up closer, joyfully slapped the parson on the shoulder, and said, "Be certain that you make good use of this, so that it will prove to be a blessing both to you and to our country. For it is silver!"

When the parson reached home again, he went first to tell his partners of the value of their find. Stopping at the innkeeper's gate, he noticed that evergreen was strewn all up the path to the door. "Who has died in this place?" he asked a boy who was leaning against the fence.

"The innkeeper himself," answered the boy. "He had drunk himself full of brandy every day for a week. He said he had found a mine and was very rich. He told everyone that now he would never have to do anything but to celebrate with drink. Last night, he drove off in his wagon—drunk as he was. Unfortunately, the wagon turned over and he was killed."

When the parson heard this, he drove homeward very distressed. He now was not quite so happy over the discovery as he had been before. When he had driven a short distance further, he saw Israel walking along the roadside. "I'll certainly be able to cheer him up with the good news that he is a rich man," the parson thought to himself. But when Israel heard that the ore was silver, he began looking more and more despondent.

"Oh no! Are you certain it's silver?" Israel kept asking again and again.

"Yes, I'm certain it's silver," the parson replied. "The expert said so himself. And I certainly would not deceive you. But why are you so sad? Are you afraid of being happy?"

"Happy?" said Israel. "Should I be happy? I figured it was only worthless glitter that we had found. So I thought it would be better to take something certain for the uncertain. I ended up selling my share to Olaf for a thousand *kronor*."[2]

Israel was in anguish. When the parson left him, Israel stood by the highway and wept.

When the parson finally reached his home, he sent a servant to tell Olaf and Eric that it was silver they had found. He decided he had had enough of passing on the "good news" himself. That evening, meditating on the day's events, the parson said to himself:

"I'll dream no more of gaining glory and profit for myself with these riches. But I can't let the silver lie buried in the earth! I must extract it for the benefit of the poor and needy. Yes, I'll work the mine and help all of the needy in the whole parish."

Two days later, the parson went out to see Olaf and his brother Eric to share with them his idea of what should be done with the silver mountain. However, when he came to their home, he discovered that neither one of them was there. A neighbor then told him to his amazement and grief that Olaf and Eric had had such a violent quarrel about the silver the previous night that Olaf had killed his brother Eric. Olaf was now in jail and would no doubt spend the

---

[2] About one hundred dollars.

rest of his life in prison. The parson went to visit Olaf in jail.

"Promise me," Olaf pleaded with the parson, "that you will watch over my children, and never let them have any portion of that silver." The parson staggered back a step and was dumbfounded.

"If you do not promise, I cannot go in peace," said Olaf. The parson pondered a moment and then said, "Yes, Olaf, I will do as you ask."

On the way home, the parson thought of the wealth that he had been so certain would bring happiness to his four companions and himself. Was it really true that the people in this community could not handle the temptation of riches? Already four men were ruined—all of whom had been wholesome and respected men in the community. He thought to himself, "If I try to mine this silver, no doubt it will destroy many others in the community. I have been appointed to watch over their souls. Is it fitting, then, for me to let loose upon them the very thing that will no doubt be their destruction? No, I can't do that."

So the next day, the parson called the peasants together to vote. He reminded them of all the misfortunes that the discovery of the silver mountain had brought upon the community already. He then asked them if they were going to let themselves be ruined further—or if they would save themselves. He also told them that they must not expect him, their spiritual adviser, to help them on their way to destruction.

"I have decided," he continued, "not to reveal to anyone where the silver mine is, and I'll never take any riches from it myself. If you wish to search for the mine and try to gain its riches, then I will move so far away from here that no word of your future misery can ever reach me. On the other hand, if you will give up thinking about the silver mine, and be content with what you have, then I'll remain as your pastor. Regardless of which way you choose, remember this: that I will never reveal the location of the silver mountain to anyone."

After talking among themselves, the peasants decided that the parson should go to the forest and conceal the vein of ore with moss and stone, so that no one would ever be able to find it — neither themselves nor their posterity.

Many years later, the country of Sweden was in a deep economic crisis, and the parson thought he should offer to tell the king the secret of the mountain. In that manner, its wealth could help the country to recover. So the pastor arranged a meeting with the king and told him the whole story of the silver mine and the events that followed its discovery.

However, when the king heard the entire story, he told the parson, "You must let the mine lie in peace. I don't want to know where it is."

"But the kingdom is in such a crisis," protested the parson. "Thousands of people are in need."

"The kingdom will surely survive this momentary crisis," the king wisely replied. "But I'm not so sure it could survive the re-discovery of your silver mountain."

The Little Hero of Holland

Mary Mapes Dodge

Many years ago, there lived a blonde-headed boy of gentle disposition in Holland. His name was Peter, and he was eight-years old. He lived in the large city of Haarlem.

Holland is a country where much of the land lies below sea level. Only great walls, called dikes, keep the fury of the North Sea from rushing in and flooding the land. For centuries, the people of Holland have worked to keep the walls strong so that their country will be safe and dry. Even the little children know that the dikes must be watched every moment, and that a hole no larger than a child's finger can be a dangerous thing.

Peter's father was one of the men who was in charge of the wooden gates in one section of the dikes. These gates are called sluices, and they are placed at regular intervals along the dikes. They regulate the amount of water going into the many canals that run across Holland.

Peter's father was responsible to either raise the sluices or lower them according to the quantity of water required. He had to carefully close the sluices at night in order to avoid any possible danger of too much water running into the canals. Otherwise, the water would soon overflow the canals and flood the surrounding countryside.

One autumn afternoon, Peter obtained his parents' consent to carry some cakes to old Mr. Jansen, a blind man who lived out in the country. Little Peter started on his errand with a light heart, and he spent an hour or so with his grateful old friend. Peter told Mr. Jansen about his walk along the dike and about the sun and flowers and the ships far out at sea. Then he remembered his mother's wish that he should return home before dark. So saying goodbye to his friend, he set out for home.

Skipping happily along the canal, he noticed how the autumn rains had swollen the waters. Even while humming different songs, he thought of his father's brave old gates and felt glad of their strength. He thought to himself, "If they gave way, where would father, mother and the rest of us be? These pretty fields would all be covered with the angry waters."

He continued to muse, "Father always calls them the 'angry waters.' I suppose that is because he thinks they are mad at him for keeping them out for so long."

And with these thoughts just flitting across his brain, the little fellow stooped to pick the pretty flowers that grew along the dike. Sometimes he stopped to throw some feathery seed ball into the air and watch it as it floated away. At other times, he listened to the stealthy rustling of a rabbit speeding through the grass. But more often he smiled as he thought about the happy light he had seen arise on the weary, listening face of his blind old friend, Mr. Jansen.

Suddenly the boy looked around him in dismay. He had not noticed that the sun was setting. Now he saw that his long shadow on the grass had vanished. It was growing dark, and he was still some distance from home. In the dim light, even the blue flowers had turned to gray. He quickened his footsteps and, with a beating heart recalled many a nursery tale of children being lost in dark, dreary forests and fields. Just as he was getting ready to run, he was startled by the sound of trickling water.

Where did it come from? He looked around and spied a small hole in the dike through which a tiny stream was flowing. Any child in Holland shudders at the thought of a leak in the dike! Peter understood the danger at once. If the water ran through a little hole, it would soon make the little hole into a larger one. And once the hole became large enough, the entire dike would collapse, and the whole city would be flooded.

Quick as a flash, he saw his duty. Throwing away his flowers, Peter clambered up the side of the dike until he reached the hole. He immediately thrust one of his fingers in the hole. It was an automatic reaction. Immediately, the trickle of water was stopped! "Ah!" he thought, with a chuckle of boyish delight. "The angry waters must stay back now! Haarlem shall not be drowned while I am here!"

This was all very well at first, but the night was falling rapidly. A damp, chilly breeze filled the air. Our little hero began to tremble with cold and dread. He shouted loudly, "Help! Come here! Come here! I need help!" But no one came. As the cold grew more intense, a numbness crept up his hand and arm—beginning with his tired finger. Soon his whole body was filled with cold and pain.

He prayed earnestly to God to send someone to help him. He shouted again, "Will no one come? Mother! Father!" Alas, his mother—the good, practical soul that she was—had already locked the doors. She fully intended to scold him the next morning for spending the night with blind old Mr. Jansen without her permission.

Peter tried to whistle. Perhaps some straggling boy might hear the signal. But his teeth chattered so, it was impossible for him to whistle. Again, he called on God for help. Although only eight years old, Peter sensed that God's answer was: "You must stay here till morning."

The midnight moon looked down upon that small, solitary form of a boy, crouched upon a stone, halfway up the dike. His head was bent, but he was not asleep. For every now and then he used his free hand to feebly rub his other arm that seemed fastened to the dike. Throughout the long night, his pale, tearful face turned with a startle at some real or fancied sound.

Peter thought of his warm bed at home, of his parents, and his brothers and sisters. But he then looked into the cold, dreary night! If he drew away that tiny finger, the angry waters—grown angrier still—would rush forth. They would never stop until they had swept over the whole city. No, he would hold his finger there until daylight—if he lived till then! He felt a strange prickling in the arm attached to the dike. It felt as though a hundred knives were pricking and piercing him from the finger in the dike up through the length of his arm. He wasn't certain now that he could draw his finger away even if he wished to! It felt glued to the dike. He continued to pray to God throughout the night.

Early the next morning, a minister who was returning from visiting a sick member of his congregation thought he heard a groan as he walked along the top of the dike. Looking over the edge, he saw Peter clinging to the side of the great wall, obviously in great agony.

"What's the matter?" the minister called. "Are you hurt?"

"I'm keeping the water back!" Peter yelled. "There's a hole in the dike. Tell the people to come quickly!"

The alarm was spread. People came running with shovels, and the hole was soon mended.

The people then carried Peter home to his parents, and before long the whole city knew how he had saved their lives that night. To this day, they have never forgotten the brave little hero of Holland.

MONI
THE GOAT BOY
Johanna Spyri

Chapter 1
All Is Well With Moni

It is a long, steep climb up to the mineral bath resort at Luzein, after leaving the road leading up through the long valley of Prattigau. The horses pant so hard on their way up the mountain that you prefer to dismount and clamber up on foot to the green summit.

After a long ascent, a person first comes to the village of Luzein, which lies on the pleasant green slopes. From there, a person can go on farther into the mountains, until the lonely buildings connected with the Resort appear, surrounded on all sides by rocky mountains. The only trees that grow up there are firs, covering the peaks and rocks. It would all look very gloomy if the delicate mountain flowers with their brilliant coloring were not peeping forth everywhere through the low pasture grass.

One clear summer evening two ladies stepped out of the mineral bath resort and went along the narrow footpath. This path begins to climb not far from the resort, and it soon becomes very steep as it ascends to the high, towering crags. At the first outcrop, the ladies stood still and looked around, for this was the very first time they had come to the mineral bath resort.

"It isn't very lively up here, Aunt," said the younger woman, as she let her eyes wander around. "There's nothing but rocks and fir woods, and then another mountain and more fir trees on it. If we're going to stay here six weeks, I should occasionally like to see something more amusing."

"It wouldn't be very amusing, in any event, if you were to lose your diamond cross up here, Paula," replied the aunt, as she tied together the red velvet ribbon from which hung the sparkling cross. "This is the third time I've fastened the ribbon since we arrived. I don't know whether it is your fault or the ribbon's, but I do know that you would be very sorry if it were lost."

"Oh, no," exclaimed Paula, decidedly, "the cross must not be lost, on any account. It came from my grandmother, and it's my greatest treasure."

Paula herself seized the ribbon, and tied two or three knots one after the other, to make it hold fast. Suddenly she pricked up her ears: "Listen, listen, Aunt, now something really lively is coming."

A merry song sounded from far above them. Then came a long, shrill yodel. Then there was singing again. The ladies looked upwards, but they couldn't see anyone. The footpath was very crooked, often passing between tall bushes and then between projecting slopes, so that from below a person could see up only a very short distance. But now there suddenly appeared someone on the slopes above, in every place where the narrow path could be seen. And the singing sounded louder and nearer.

"See, see, Aunt, there! Over there! Look!" exclaimed Paula with great delight. Before the aunt was even aware of it, three—then four—goats came bounding down, and then more and more of them. Each goat was wearing a little bell around its neck, so that the sound came from every direction. In the midst of the flock came the goat boy skipping along, and singing his song to the very end:

And in winter I am happy,
For weeping is in vain,
And, besides, the glad springtime
Will soon come again.

Then he gave a loud yodel, and he immediately stood before the ladies with his flock. For with his bare feet, he leaped as nimbly and lightly as his little goats.

"I wish you good evening!" he said pleasantly as he looked at the two ladies. He would have continued on his way, but the ladies were delighted with the goat boy and his merry eyes.

"Wait a minute," said Paula. "Are you the goat boy of Luzein? Do the goats belong to the village below?"

"As a matter of fact, I am!" Moni replied. "And, yes, most of the goats belong to the villagers below."

"Do you go up there with them every day?"

"Yes, surely."

"Is that so? And what is your name?"

"My name is Moni."

"Will you sing me the song once more—the one that you have just sung? We heard only one verse."

"I would like to," explained Moni, "but it is a very long song. And it would be too late for the goats, for they must go home at once." He straightened his weather-beaten cap and swung his staff in the air. The goats had already begun to nibble all around, and so he called to them: "Home! Home!"

"You will sing to me some other time, Moni, won't you?" called Paula after him.

"Yes, I will, and good night!" he called back, then trotted along with the goats. In a short time, the whole flock stood still below. The goats were just a few steps from the mineral bath resort by the rear building. For here Moni had to leave the three goats belonging to the resort: the beautiful white one and the black one with the pretty little kid named Maggie. Moni treated Maggie with great care, for she was a delicate little creature, and he loved her more than all the others. Maggie was so attached to him that she ran after him continually all day long. He now led her very tenderly along and placed her in her shed. Then he said:

"There, Maggie, now sleep well. Are you tired? It is really a long way up the mountain, and you are still so little. Now lie right down in the nice straw!"

After he had put Maggie to bed in this way, he hurried along with the rest of the flock—first up to the hill in front of the Baths, and then down the road to the village.

When he reached the village, Moni took out his little horn and blew so vigorously that it resounded far across the valley. From all the scattered houses, the children now came running out. Each rushed upon his goat, which he recognized a long way off. And from the houses nearby, one woman and then another seized her little goat by the cord or the horns. In a short time, the entire flock was separated and each goat went to its own place. Finally Moni stood alone with the brown one, his own goat. With her he now went to the little house on the side of the mountain. His grandmother was waiting for him in the doorway.

"Has all gone well today, Moni?" she asked pleasantly. He assured her that it had. She then led the brown goat to her shed and immediately began to milk her. The grandmother was still a robust woman and personally looked after everything in both the house and the shed. The whole lot was in nicely kept order. Moni stood in the doorway of the shed and watched his grandmother. When the milking was ended, she went into the little house and said: "Come, Moni, you must be hungry."

She had everything already prepared. Moni had only to sit down at the table. She seated herself next to him. Moni enjoyed his supper tremendously even though there was nothing on the table but a bowl of cornmeal mush cooked with milk from the family goat. As they ate, Moni told his grandmother what he had done throughout the day. As soon as the meal was ended, he went straight to bed. For in the early dawn he would have to start out again with the flock.

Moni had already spent many summers in this manner. He had been a goat boy so long and had become so accustomed to this life, that he could think of nothing else. Moni had lived with his grandmother ever since he could remember. His mother had died when he was still very little. His father soon after went with others to military service in Naples—in order to earn a decent living, as he said. For he thought he could get better pay there.

Moni's grandmother was also poor, but she took her daughter's deserted baby boy, Moni, home at once and shared what she had with him. He brought a blessing to her cottage, and she had never suffered any need.

Good old Elizabeth was very popular with everyone in the whole village. So when a new goat boy had to be appointed to take the village goats to the mountain pastures, Moni was chosen with one accord. Everyone was glad for the hard-working Elizabeth that now Moni would be able to earn something to help the household. The pious grandmother had never let Moni start away a single morning, without reminding him:

"Moni, never forget how near you are up there to the dear Lord, and that He sees and hears everything. You can hide nothing from His eyes. But never forget, either, that He is near to help you. So you have nothing to fear. And if you can call upon no human being up there, you only have to call to the dear Lord in your need. For He will hear you immediately and come to your aid."

So from the very first, Moni went up to the lonely mountains and the highest crags full of trust, and he never had the slightest fear or dread. For he always thought:

"The higher up, the nearer I am to the dear Lord, and so all the safer whatever may happen."

So Moni had neither care nor trouble and could enjoy everything he did from morning till night. It was no wonder that he whistled and sang and yodeled continually, for he had to express his great happiness.

Chapter 2
Moni's Life In The Mountains

The following morning Paula awoke earlier than ever before. A loud singing had awakened her out of her sleep.

"That's surely the goat boy so early in the morning," she said, springing out of bed and running to the window.

Quite right. With fresh red cheeks there stood Moni below, and he had just brought the old goat and the little kid out of the goat shed. Now he swung his staff in the air, and the goats leaped and sprang around him. He then walked along with the whole flock. Suddenly Moni raised his voice again and sang until the mountains echoed:

Up yonder in the fir trees
Sing the birds in a choir,
And after the rain comes,
Comes the sun like a fire.

"Today I must have him sing his whole song for me," Paula said. For Moni had now disappeared, and she could no longer make out the words of his distant song.

In the sky the rosy morning clouds were disappearing, and a cool mountain breeze rustled around Moni's ears as he climbed. Moni enjoyed this, and he yodeled so heartily with satisfaction from the first ledge down into the valley that many of the sleepers in the mineral bath resort below opened their eyes in amazement. They then closed them again at once, for they recognized the sound. They knew that they could have an hour longer to sleep—since the goat boy always came so early. Meanwhile Moni climbed with his goats for an hour longer, farther and farther up to the high cliffs above.

The higher up he mounted, the broader and more beautiful became the view. From time to time, he looked around him, then gazed up into the bright sky, which was becoming bluer and bluer. He then began to sing with all his might. The higher he climbed, the louder and more merrily he sang:

Up yonder in the fir trees
Sing the birds in a choir.
And after the rain falls,
The sun comes like a fire.

And the sun and the stars
And the moon in the night,
The dear Lord has made them
To give us delight.

In the spring there are flowers.
They are yellow and gold,
And so blue is the sky then
My joy can't be told.

And in summer there are berries,
There are plenty if it's fine,
And the red ones and black ones,
I eat them all from the vine.

If there are nuts in the bushes
I know what to do.

Where the goats like to nibble,
There I can hunt too.

And in winter I'm happy,
For weeping is in vain.
And besides, the glad springtime
Will soon come again."

Moni finally reached the place where he usually stayed. He planned to remain there for a while today. It was a little green tableland, with so broad an outcrop that one could see from the top all around and far, far down into the valley. This outcrop was called Pulpit Rock. Here Moni often stayed for hours at a time, gazing about him and whistling away—while his little goats quite contentedly sought their food around him.

As soon as Moni arrived, he took his provision bag from his back and laid it in a little hole in the ground that he had dug out for this very purpose. He then went to Pulpit Rock and threw himself on the grass in order to enjoy himself fully.

The sky had now become a deep blue. Above Moni were the high mountains with peaks towering to the sky and great ice fields shimmering in the sun. The morning light shone far away down below into the emerald green valley. Moni lay there, looking about, singing and whistling. The mountain wind cooled his warm face. And as soon as he stopped whistling, the birds chirped all the more heartily and flew up into the blue sky. Moni was indescribably happy.

From time to time, Maggie came to Moni and rubbed her head on his shoulder out of sheer affection, as she often did. Then she bleated quite fondly, went to Moni's other side and rubbed her head on his other shoulder. The other goats also—first one and then another—came to look at their shepherd. Each had her own way of paying him a visit.

The brown one, which Moni owned, came very cautiously and looked at him to see if he was all right. She would then stand and gaze at him until he said: "Yes, yes, Braunli, it's all right. Go and look for your food."

The young white one and Swallow rushed together upon Moni so energetically that they would have knocked him down if he had not already been stretched out on the ground. Swallow was given her name because she was small and nimble. She darted everywhere, like swallows into their holes. After greeting Moni in this fashion, the two goats immediately darted off again.

Maggie's mother, named Blackie, belonged to the landlord of the mineral bath resort. Blackie had a shiny coat and was a little proud. She came only to within a few steps of Moni. She looked at him with her head lifted, as if she didn't want to appear too familiar. She then went her way again. Big Sultan, the billy goat, only showed himself one time. He then pushed away all the goats he found near Moni. He bleated loudly several times as if he had information to give Moni about the condition of the flock. For he considered himself to be the flock's real shepherd.

Only little Maggie never allowed herself to be crowded away from her protector. If the billy goat came and tried to push her aside, she crept so far under Moni's arm or head that big Sultan no longer came near her. And so under Moni's protection, the little kid was not the least bit afraid of Sultan. Otherwise she would have trembled if he came near her.

In this manner, the sunny morning had passed. Moni had already taken his midday meal and now stood thinking as he leaned upon his staff. He often needed his staff, for it was very useful in climbing up and down. He was now pondering whether he should go up to a new side of the rocks, for he wanted to go higher with the goats this afternoon. But the question was, to which side? Finally, he decided to take the left. In that direction were the three Dragon Stones, around which grew such tender shrubs that it was a real feast for the goats.

The way was steep, and there were dangerous places in the rugged wall of rock. But he knew a good path, and the goats were sensible and did not easily go astray. He began to climb, and all his goats gaily clambered after him—some in front, some behind him. Little Maggie always stayed quite close to him. Occasionally he held her tight and pulled her along with him when he came to a very steep place.

All went quite well, and soon they were at the top. With high bounds, the goats ran immediately to the green bushes. For they knew quite well how good the feasting would be, as they had often nibbled up here before.

"Be quiet! Be quiet!" commanded Moni, "Don't push each other to the steep places, for in a moment one of you might go down and have your legs broken. Swallow! Swallow! What are you thinking of?" he anxiously called up to the goat. For the nimble

Swallow had climbed up to the high Dragon Stones and was now standing on the outermost edge of one of them, looking down on him quite brazenly. He climbed up quickly, for only a single step more and Swallow would be lying below at the foot of the precipice. Moni was very agile, and in a few minutes he had climbed up on the crag, quickly seized Swallow by the leg, and pulled her down.

"Now come with me, you foolish little beast, you," scolded Moni, as he dragged Swallow along with him to the others. He held her tight for a while, until she had taken a good bite of a shrub and thought no more of running away.

"Where is Maggie?" Moni suddenly shouted, as he noticed Blackie standing alone in a steep place. Rather than eating, she was quietly looking around her. Moni was quite concerned, for little Maggie was normally either near Moni or running after her mother.

"What have you done with your little kid, Blackie?" he called in alarm as he rushed towards the goat. Blackie was acting strangely. Instead of eating, she just stood still in the same spot and pricked up her ears inquiringly. Moni placed himself beside her and looked up and down. Suddenly he heard a faint, pitiful bleating. It was Maggie's voice, and it came so plaintively and beseechingly from below.

Moni lay down on the ground and leaned over. There below he saw something moving. Getting a better look, he could see quite plainly that far below Maggie was hanging on to the bough of a tree which grew out of the rock. She was moaning pitifully. Evidently, she had fallen over. Fortunately the bough had caught her, otherwise she would have fallen into the ravine and met a sad death. Even now if she could no longer hold to the bough, she would fall into the depths and be dashed to pieces.

In the greatest anguish, he called down: "Stay still, Maggie, don't try to move! Look, I'm coming to get you!"

But how could he reach there? Moni saw very well that it would be impossible to go straight down after her. That's because the wall of rock was too steep where he was standing. But the little goat must be down there somewhere near the Rain Rock. That was the name he and the other goat boys had given to the overhanging stone under which good protection was to be found in rainy weather. The goat boys had always spent rainy days there, since olden times. Moni felt that from there he could climb across over the rocks and rescue the little kid.

He quickly whistled the flock together and went with them down to the place from which he could reach the Rain Rock. There he left them to graze while he went on to the rock itself. From the top of the Rain Rock, Moni immediately saw the bough of the tree just a little bit above him—and the kid balanced on it precariously. He realized that it would not be an easy task to climb up there and then back down again with Maggie on his back. Yet, there was no other way to rescue her. And he was convinced the dear Lord would surely stand by him. With God's help, he felt he could not possibly fail. He folded his hands, looked up to heaven and prayed: "Oh, dear Lord, help me so that I can save Maggie!"

Then, full of trust that all would go well, he bravely clambered up the rock until he reached the tree limb above. Here he clung fast with both feet, lifted the trembling, moaning little creature to his shoulders, and then climbed with great caution back down again. When he had the firm earth under his feet once more and had saved the terror-stricken kid, he was so glad he had to offer thanks aloud. He cried up to heaven:

"Oh, dear Lord, I thank you a thousand times for having helped us so well! Oh, we are both so glad for it!" Then he sat down on the ground a little while and stroked the kid. She was still trembling in all her delicate limbs, and Moni comforted her for enduring so much suffering.

As it was soon time to depart, Moni placed the little goat on his shoulders again, and said softly: "Come, poor Maggie, you are still trembling. You cannot walk home today. I must carry you." And so he carried the little creature, clinging close to him, all the way down.

Paula was standing on the last rise in front of the mineral bath resort, waiting for the goat boy. Her aunt had accompanied her. When Moni came down with Maggie on his back, Paula showed great concern and wanted to know if the kid was sick. When Moni saw this, he at once sat down on the ground in front of Paula and told her his day's experience with Maggie.

The young lady showed very keen interest in the affair and stroked the little rescued creature, which now lay quietly in Moni's lap. The kid looked very pretty with its white feet and the beautiful black coat on its back. She was very willing to be stroked by Paula.

"Now sing your song again for me while you're sitting here," Paula said. Moni was in such a happy frame of mind that he willingly and heartily sang his entire song from beginning to end.

This pleased Paula exceptionally well and she said he must sing it to her often again. Then they all went together down to the mineral bath resort. Here the kid was laid in her bed, and Moni said farewell. Paula went back to her room to talk with her aunt longer about the goat boy, whose merry song she had enjoyed again.

Chapter 3
A Visit

In this manner, many days passed by, one as sunny and clear as the other. For it was an unusually beautiful summer, and the sky remained blue and cloudless from morning till evening.

Early every morning without exception the goat boy went by the mineral bath resort, singing heartily. Every evening he came back again singing with gusto. All the guests were so accustomed to the merry sound that no one would have willingly missed it.

More than all the others, Paula delighted in Moni's joyfulness, and she went out almost every evening to meet and talk with him.

One sunny morning Moni had once more reached Pulpit Rock, and he was about to lay down on it. However, he suddenly changed his mind. "No, go on!" he told the goats. "The last time you had to leave all the nice little plants because we had to go after Maggie. Now we will go up there again, so that you can finish nibbling them!"

The goats all leaped with delight after him, for they knew they were going up to the lovely bushes on the Dragon Stones. Today Moni closely held his little Maggie in his arms the whole time. He pulled the sweet plants from the rocks himself and let her eat out of his hand. This pleased the little goat best of all. She rubbed her head quite contentedly from time to time against Moni's shoulder and bleated happily. So the whole morning passed before Moni noticed—from his own hunger—that it had grown late before he was aware of it. But he had left his lunch below in the little hole near Pulpit Rock, for he had intended to return again at noon.

"Well, you've had your fill of good things, and I've had nothing," he said to his goats. "Now I must eat something too, and you'll find enough down below. Come along!" With that, he gave a loud whistle, and the whole flock began moving down the mountain, the liveliest ones always ahead. In fact, first of all was light-footed Swallow, who was to meet something unexpected today. She sprang down from stone to stone and across many a cleft in the rocks, but all at once she could go no farther. Directly in front of her suddenly stood a chamois, who gazed with curiosity into her face.

This had never happened to Swallow before! She stood still and looked questioningly at this stranger. She waited for the chamois to get out of her way so she could leap to the next boulder, as she intended. But the chamois didn't stir and gazed boldly into Swallow's eyes. So they stood facing each other, more and more obstinate.

They might have stood there until now, if big Sultan had not come along in the meantime. As soon as he saw the state of things, he stepped quite considerately past Swallow and suddenly pushed the chamois aside so far and with such violence, that she had to make a daring leap to avoid falling down over the rocks. Swallow went triumphantly on her way, and Sultan marched proudly and contentedly behind her, for he felt himself to be the sure protector of the goats in his flock.

Meanwhile Moni (coming down from above) and another goat boy (coming up from below) met at the same spot and looked at each other in astonishment. However, they were well acquainted, and after getting over their surprise, they greeted each other cordially. It was Jorgli from the nearby town of St. Anthony. Half the morning he had been looking in vain for Moni, and now he met him up here—where he hadn't expected to find him.

"I didn't realize you came up so high with the goats," Jorgli said.

"Sometimes I do," replied Moni, "but not always. Usually I stay by Pulpit Rock and around there. Why have *you* come up here?"

"To make you a visit," was the reply. "I have something to tell you. Besides, I have two goats here, that I am bringing to the landlord at the mineral bath resort. He's going to buy one, and so I thought I would come up to see you."

"Are they your own goats?" asked Moni.

"Of course they're ours. I don't tend strange ones any longer. I'm not a goat boy now."

Moni was very much surprised at this, for Jorgli had become the goat boy of St. Anthony at the same time that Moni had been made goat boy of Luzein. Moni couldn't understand how Jorgli could give it up without a single murmur.

Meanwhile the goat boys and their flocks had reached Pulpit Rock. Moni brought out bread and a small piece of dried meat and invited Jorgli to share his midday meal. They both sat down on Pulpit Rock and ate heartily, for it had grown very late and they had hungry appetites. When everything was eaten and they had drunk a little goat's milk, Jorgli comfortably stretched himself at full length on the ground and rested his head on both arms. However, Moni remained sitting, for he always liked to look down into the deep valley below.

"But what are you doing for work now, Jorgli, if you're no longer a goat boy?" began Moni. "You must be working somewhere."

"Of course I have a job," replied Jorgli, "and a very good one. I'm an egg boy now. Every day I carry eggs to all the hotels, as far as I can go. I come up here to the mineral bath resort, too. Yesterday I was there."

Moni shook his head. "That's nothing. I wouldn't be an egg boy. I would a thousand times rather be a goat boy. I think it's much finer."

"Why do you say that?"

"Eggs aren't alive. You can't speak to them, and they don't run after you like goats—which are glad to see you when you come. Goats are fond of you, and they understand every word you say to them. You can't possibly have the same pleasure with eggs as you can with the goats up here."

"Yes, and you," interrupted Jorgli testily, "what great pleasure do you have up here? Just now you've had to get up six times while we were eating, just on account of that silly kid, to prevent her from falling down below. Is that really a pleasure?"

"Yes, I like to do that! Isn't it so, Maggie? Come! Come here!" Moni jumped up and ran after the kid, for she was making dangerous leaps for sheer joy.

When he sat down again, Jorgli said: "There is another way to keep the young goats from falling over the rocks, without having to be always jumping after them, as you do."

"What is it?" asked Moni.

"Drive a stick firmly into the ground and fasten the goat by the leg to it. She will kick furiously, but she can't get away."

"You needn't think I would do any such thing to the little kid!" said Moni quite angrily. He quickly drew Maggie to him and held her tightly, as if to protect her from any such treatment.

"You really won't have to take care of that one much longer," began Jorgli again. "She won't come up here many more times."

"What? What? What did you say, Jorgli?" demanded Moni.

"Hah, don't you know about it? The landlord won't continue to raise her. She's too weak. In fact, there never was a more feeble goat. He wanted to sell her to my father, but my father wouldn't have her either. So now the landlord is going to have her killed next week, and then he will buy our spotted goat."

Moni had become quite pale from terror. At first he couldn't speak a word, but now he broke out and exclaimed aloud over the little kid:

"No, no, that shall *not* be done, Maggie, it shall *not* be done. They shall not slaughter you. I can't bear that. Oh, I would rather die with you. No, this just cannot be!"

"Don't carry on so," said Jorgli, angrily, as he pulled Moni up. (In his grief, Moni had thrown himself face down on the ground.)

"Stand up! You know the kid really belongs to the landlord, and he can do what he likes with her. Think no more about it! Come, I know something. Look what I have!" Jorgli now held out one hand to Moni. It had something in it, but with the other hand, Jorgli almost covered the object so that Moni could barely see it. It sparkled wonderfully in his hand, for the sun shone straight onto it.

"What is it?" asked Moni, when it sparkled again, being lit up by a sunbeam.

"Guess!"

"A ring?"

"No, but something like that."

"Who gave it to you?"

"Gave it to me? Nobody. I found it myself."

"Then it doesn't belong to you, Jorgli."

"Why not? I didn't take it from anybody. In fact, I almost stepped on it with my foot, and then it would have been broken. So I can just as well keep it."

"Where did you find it?"

"Down by the mineral bath resort, yesterday evening."

"Then someone from the resort below lost it. You must tell the landlord at once. If you don't, I will do it this evening."

"No, no, Moni, don't do that," said Jorgli, beseechingly. "See, I will show you what it is, and I will sell it to a maid in one of the hotels. Surely she will give me at least four francs for it. Then I will give you one or two, and nobody will know anything about it."

"I won't take it! I won't take it!" interrupted Moni hotly. "And the dear Lord has heard everything you've said."

Jorgli looked up to the sky: "Oh, so far away," he said skeptically. But he immediately began to speak more softly.

"He hears you still," said Moni confidently.

It was no longer Jorgli's secret. If he didn't know how to bring Moni to his side, all would be lost. He thought and thought.

"Moni," he said suddenly, "I will promise you something that will delight you—if you will not say anything to anyone about what I have found. You really don't need to take anything for it, then you will have nothing to do with it. If you will do as I say, I'll make sure my father buys Maggie, so she won't be killed. Will you?"

A hard struggle arose in Moni. He knew it was wrong to help keep the discovery secret. But ...

Jorgli now opened his hand. In it lay a cross set with a large number of stones, which sparkled in many colors. Moni realized that it was not a worthless thing that no one would inquire about. He felt that if he remained silent it was exactly as if he himself were keeping what did not belong to him. But on the other hand, there was the little, affectionate Maggie. She was going to be killed in a horrible way with a knife, and he could prevent it if he kept silent.

Even now the little kid was lying so trustfully beside him, as if she knew that he would always keep her safe. No, he could not let her be killed. He must try to save her.

"Yes, I will, Jorgli," he said, but without any enthusiasm.

"Then it's a deal!" Jorgli said as he offered his hand to Moni so that he might seal the agreement. For that was the only way to make a promise binding, according to the custom there.

Jorgli was very glad that now his secret was safe. He thought it would be a good idea to start towards home with his two goats. Jorgli had much farther to go to reach home than Moni, and Moni had now become very quiet. So he said goodnight to Moni and whistled for his two goats—who had meanwhile joined Moni's grazing goats. However, there had been quite a bit of pushing and other doubtful behavior between the two groups of goats. The goats from Luzein had never heard that they ought to be polite to visitors. And the goats from St. Anthony didn't know that they ought not to seek out the best plants or push the others away from them when they were visiting. After Jorgli had gone some distance down the mountain, Moni also started along with his flock. However, he was very quiet and neither sang a note nor whistled all the way home.

Chapter 4

Moni Can No Longer Sing

The next morning, Moni came up the path to the mineral bath resort, just as silent and downcast as the evening before. He brought out the landlord's goats quietly and went on upwards, but he didn't sing a note, nor did he give a yodel up into the air. He let his head hang, and he looked as if he were afraid of something. Now and then he looked around timidly, as if someone were coming after him to question him.

Moni could no longer be merry. He himself didn't know exactly why. He wanted to be glad that he had saved Maggie and be able to sing. But somehow he couldn't express it. Today the sky was covered with clouds. Moni thought that perhaps when the sun came out it would be different, and he could be happy again.

However, when Moni reached the top, it began to rain quite hard. He took refuge under the Rain Rock, for it soon poured in streams from the sky. The goats came, too, and placed themselves here and there under the rock. The aristocratic Blackie immediately wanted to protect her beautiful shiny coat, and she crept in under the rock before Moni did. She was now standing behind Moni and looking out from her comfortable corner into the pouring rain.

Maggie was standing in front of her protector under the projecting rock, and she gently rubbed her little head against his knee. Then she looked up at him in surprise, because Moni didn't say a word. And she wasn't accustomed to that. Moni sat thoughtfully, leaning on his staff. For in such weather, he always held it in his hand to keep himself from slipping on the steep places. Now, as he sat for hours under the Rain Rock, he had plenty of time for reflection.

Moni thought over what he had promised Jorgli. It seemed to him that if Jorgli was guilty of taking something, he was practically doing the same thing himself. That's because Jorgli had promised to do something for him if Moni kept quiet. Moni had surely done what was wrong, and the dear Lord was now against him. This he felt in his heart, and it was right that it was dark and rainy and that he was hidden under the rock. For he would not even have dared look up into the blue sky as usual.

But there were still other things that Moni had to think about. If Maggie should fall down over a steep precipice again, and he wanted to get her, the dear Lord perhaps would no longer protect him. And Moni no longer dared to pray to Him about it and call upon Him, and so he had no more sense of safety. And what if he should slip and fall down with Maggie deep over the jagged rocks? What if both of them should lie all torn and maimed?

Oh, no, he said with anguish in his heart. He could not let that happen. He must manage to be able to pray again and come to the dear Lord with everything that weighed on his heart. Only then could he be happy again. Of that, he felt certain. Yes, Moni *would* throw off the weight that oppressed him. He *would* go and tell the landlord everything. But then what? Then Jorgli would not persuade his father to buy Maggie, and then the landlord would slaughter Maggie. Oh, no! Oh, no! He couldn't bear that. So he said to himself: "No, I won't do it! I will say nothing!" But he didn't feel satisfied, and the weight on his heart grew heavier and heavier. Thus Moni's whole day passed.

He started home at evening as silent as he had come in the morning. When he came near the mineral bath resort, he saw Paula standing there. She quickly dashed over to the goat shed and asked sympathetically: "Moni, what's the matter? Why don't you sing anymore?"

He turned shyly away and mumbled: "I can't." He then quickly made off with his goats.

Paula later said to her aunt, "If I only knew what was the matter with the goat boy! He is quite changed. You wouldn't know him. If he would only sing again!"

"It must be the frightful rain that has silenced the boy so!" remarked the aunt.

"Everything is going wrong. Let's go home, Aunt," Paula begged. "There's no more pleasure here. First I lost my beautiful cross, and it can't be found. Then comes this endless rain, and now we can't ever hear the merry goat boy any more. Let's go away!"

"The cure must be finished, or it will do no good," explained the aunt. "I must continue to take the mineral baths as was prescribed." It was also dark and gray on the following day, and the rain poured down without ceasing. Moni spent this day exactly like the one before. He sat under the rock, and his thoughts went restlessly around in a circle.

He would say to himself, "Now, I will go and confess the wrong, so that I shall dare to look up to the dear Lord again." But then he pictured the little kid under the knife before him, and the turmoil began all over again in his mind. So with all this thinking and brooding—and with the weight of emotion he carried—he was very tired by nightfall. He silently crept down the mountain in the streaming rain as if he didn't notice it at all.

When Moni reached the mineral bath resort below, the landlord was standing in the back doorway. He called out to Moni: "Hurry in with the goats. They are wet enough! You've been crawling down the mountain like a snail! What's the matter with you?"

The landlord had never been so unfriendly before. In fact, he had always made very friendly remarks to the merry goat boy. But he was upset with Moni's behavior. Besides he was in a worse humor than usual because Paula had just complained to him about the loss of her cross. She had assured him that the valuable cross could only have been lost inside the resort or directly in front of the entrance to the building. She knew that because she had only stepped out once on the day it was lost. And that was to hear the goat boy sing on his way home that evening.

Of course it made the landlord angry to hear that such a costly thing had been lost beyond recovery in his resort. In fact, the day before he had called together the whole staff of servants. He closely questioned each one of them and threatened them if the guilty party didn't come forward. However, it was to no avail. Finally, he offered a reward to the finder. The whole house was in an uproar over the lost cross.

The next day, when Moni with his goats passed by the front of the house, Paula was standing there. She had been waiting for him because she wondered very much whether he would ever sing any more or be merry again. As he now crept by, she called: "Moni! Moni! Are you really the same goat boy who used to sing from morning till night:

And so blue is the sky there
My joy can't be told?"

Moni heard the words, but he gave no answer. Nevertheless, Paula's words made a great impression on him. Oh, how different things really were from the time when he could sing all day long—and when the song matched his feelings exactly. Oh, if it could only be like that once more!

Again Moni climbed up the mountain, silent and sad, without singing. The rain had now ceased, but thick fog hung around on the mountains. The sky was still full of dark clouds. Moni again sat under the rock and battled with his thoughts. About noon the sky began to clear. It grew brighter and brighter. Moni came out of his cave and looked around. The goats once more sprang gaily here and there, and the little kid was quite frolicsome from delight at the returning sun. She made the merriest of leaps.

Moni stood on Pulpit Rock, and he saw how it was growing brighter and more beautiful in the valley below. Likewise, it was growing brighter over the mountains beyond. Soon the clouds scattered, and the lovely light blue sky looked cheerful. It seemed to Moni as if the dear Lord were looking out of the bright blue at him, and suddenly it became quite clear in his heart what he ought to do. He could not carry the wrong around with him anymore. He must throw it off.

Quickly Moni seized the little kid, who was jumping about him, took her in his arms and said tenderly: "Oh, Maggie, you poor Maggie! I have certainly done what I could. But it is wrong, and I mustn't do it any longer. Oh, if only you didn't have to die! I can't bear it!"

And Moni began to cry so hard that he could no longer speak. The kid bleated pitifully and crept far under his arm, as if she wanted to cling to him and be protected. Then Moni lifted the little goat on his shoulders, saying: "Come, Maggie, I will carry you home once more today. Perhaps I can't carry you much longer."

When the flock came down to the mineral bath resort, Paula was again waiting for him. Moni put the young goat with her mother in the shed, and instead of going on farther, he came toward Paula and started going past her into the resort. However, she stopped him.

"Still no singing, Moni? Where are you going with such a troubled face?"

"I have to tell the landlord about something," replied Moni, without lifting his eyes.

"Tell him about something? What is it? Can't I know?"

"I must tell the landlord himself. Something has been found."

"Found? What is it? I have lost something—a beautiful cross."

"Yes, that is just what it is."

"What did you say?" exclaimed Paula, in the greatest surprise. "Is it a cross with sparkling stones?"

"Yes, exactly that."

"What have you done with it, Moni? Give it to me. Did you find it?"

"No, Jorgli from St. Anthony found it."

Then Paula wanted to know who Jorgli was and where he lived, and to send someone to St. Anthony at once to get the cross.

"I will go as fast as I can, and if he still has it I will bring it to you," said Moni.

"If he still has it?" said Paula. "Why shouldn't he still have it? And how do you know all about it, Moni? When did he find it, and how did you hear about it?"

Moni looked on the ground. He didn't dare say how it had all come about and how he had helped to conceal the discovery until he could no longer bear it.

But Paula was very kind to Moni. She took him aside, sat down beside him on the trunk of a tree and said with the greatest friendliness: "Come, tell me all about how it happened, Moni, for I want so much to know everything from you."

Then Moni gained his confidence and began to relate the whole story. He told her every word of his struggle about Maggie and how he had lost all happiness. He admitted he dared no longer look up to the dear Lord and that today he finally couldn't bear it any longer.

Then Paula talked with him very kindly and said he should have come immediately and told everything. She also told him it was right that he had told her everything now so openly. She assured him that he would not regret it. Then she said he could promise Jorgli ten francs as soon as she had the cross in her hands again.

"Ten francs!" repeated Moni, full of astonishment. For he knew Jorgli had planned to sell it for much less. Then Moni jumped up and said he would go that very evening to St. Anthony. He promised that if he got the cross he would bring it with him early the next morning. He ran along and was once more able to leap and jump. He now had a much lighter heart, and the heavy burden no longer weighed him down.

When Moni reached home, he quickly put his goats in and told his grandmother he had an errand to do. At once he ran down to St. Anthony. He found Jorgli at home and told him without delay what he had done. At first the boy was very angry, but when he realized that the whole story was out, he took out the cross and asked: "Will she give me anything for it?"

"Yes, and now you can see, Jorgli," said Moni indignantly, "how by being honorable you will receive ten francs. By being deceitful, you would have only received four. You're going to have the ten francs as soon as I return the cross."

Jorgli was very much amazed. He regretted that he had not gone immediately with the cross to the mineral bath resort after he had picked it up in front of the door. For he would never have a clear conscience about it. Yet, it might have all been so different if he had just done the right thing! He gave the cross to Moni, who rushed home with it, for it had already grown quite dark.

Chapter 5
Moni Sings Again

Paula had asked the staff to awaken her early the next morning, for she wanted to be right there when the goat boy came. She was anxious to speak with him herself. That evening she had conversed at length with the landlord, and when she left his room she was quite joyful. So she must have planned something delightful with him.

When Moni came along with his flock in the morning, Paula was already standing in front of the hotel, and she called out: "Moni, can you still not sing?"

He shook his head. "No, I can't. I am always wondering how much longer Maggie will go with me. I never can sing any more as long as I live, but here is the cross you lost." With that, he handed her a little package. For his grandmother had wrapped the cross carefully for him in three or four papers.

Paula took out the cross from the wrappings and examined it closely. It really was her beautiful cross with the sparkling stones, and it was quite unharmed. "Well, Moni," she said very kindly, "you have given me great pleasure. If it had not been for you, I might never have seen my cross again. Now, I want to make you joyful as well. Go take Maggie out of the shed, for she belongs to you now!"

Moni stared at the young lady in astonishment, as if it were impossible to grasp her words. At last he stammered: "But how—how can Maggie be mine?"

"How?" replied Paula, smiling. "Well, last evening I bought her from the landlord, and this morning I'm giving her to you. Now can't you sing once more?"

"Oh! My!" exclaimed Moni and ran like mad to the shed, led the little goat out, and took her in his arms. Then he leaped back and held out his hand to Paula and said over and over again:

"I thank you a thousand, thousand times! May God bless you! If only I could do something nice for you!"

"Well then, try once more and let's see if you can sing again!" Paula said.

Then Moni sang his song and went on up the mountain with the goats. His jubilant tones rang down into the valley, so that there was no one in the whole mineral bath resort who did not hear it. Many a person turned over in his bed and said: "The goat boy has good weather once more." All were glad to hear him singing again, for all of them had depended on his merry alarm—some in order to get up, others to sleep a while longer.

When Moni reached the first summit, he saw Paula still standing below in front of the hotel. He stepped as far out as possible and sang down at the top of his voice:

And so blue is the sky there
My joy can't be told.

The whole day long Moni shouted for joy, and all the goats caught his spirit and jumped and sprang around as if it were a great festival. The sun shone cheerfully down out of the blue sky. After the great rain, all the little plants were so fresh, and the yellow and red flowers were particularly bright. It seemed to Moni as if he had never seen the mountains and the valley and the whole world so beautiful before. He didn't let the little kid leave him the whole day. He pulled up the best plants for her and fed her, and said over and over again: "Maggie, you dear Maggie, you don't have to die after all. You're now mine and will come up to the pasture with me as long as you live."

And with resounding singing and yodeling, Moni came down again at evening. After he had led the black goat to her shed, he took the little kid in his arms, for she was now coming home with him. Maggie didn't protest, but pressed close to Moni and felt that she was under the best protection. After all, Moni had for a long time treated Maggie better and more kindly than her own mother.

When Moni came near his grandmother's house with Maggie on his shoulders, his grandmother didn't know at all what to make of it. Even though Moni called from a distance: "She belongs to me, Grandmother, she belongs to me!" she didn't understand for some time what he meant.

But Moni couldn't explain it to her quite yet. He ran to the shed and made Maggie a fine, soft bed of fresh straw. He made the bed next to Brownie, so that she wouldn't be afraid. As he laid down the little kid, he said, "There, Maggie, now sleep well in your new home! You will always have this. Every day I will make you a new bed!"

Then Moni came back to his wondering grandmother, and while they sat together at their supper, he told her the whole story from the very beginning about his three days so full of trouble, and the happy ending today. His grandmother listened very quietly and attentively and when he came to the end, she said earnestly:

"Moni, you must remember what has happened to you now, as long as you live! While you were having so much trouble with wrongdoing in order to help the little creature, the dear Lord had already found a way to help her and make you happy as soon as you would do what was right in His sight. If you had done right at the very start and trusted in God, all would have gone well from the beginning. Now the dear Lord has helped you beyond all you deserved, so that you will not forget it your whole life long."

"No, I will surely never forget it," said Moni, eagerly agreeing. "And from now on, I will always truly think from the very start: I must only do what is right before the dear Lord. He will take care of all the rest."

Before Moni could lie down to sleep, he had to look into the shed once more, to see if it were really possible that the little kid was lying out there and belonged to him.

Jorgli received the ten francs according to the agreement, but he was not allowed to escape from the affair as easily as that. When he returned to the mineral bath resort, he was brought to the landlord, who took the boy by the collar and said threateningly:

"Jorgli! Jorgli! Don't you try a second time to bring my hotel into bad repute! If anything like this ever happens again, you will come out of my hotel in a way that will not please you! See, up there hangs a very sharp willow rod for such cases. Now go and think this over."

Not only that, the event had other consequences for Jorgli. From that time on, if anything was lost anywhere in the mineral bath resort, all the servants immediately exclaimed: "Jorgli from St. Anthony has it!" And if he came afterwards into the hotel, they all pounced on him together and cried: "Give it here, Jorgli! Out with it!" And if he assured them he had nothing and knew nothing about it, they would all exclaim: "We know all about you already! You can't fool us!"

So Jorgli had to endure the most menacing attacks continually, and had hardly a moment's peace any more. For if he saw any one approaching him, he at once thought the person was coming to ask if he had found this or that. So Jorgli was not at all happy. A hundred times he thought to himself: "If only I had given back that cross immediately! I will never in my whole life keep anything else that doesn't belong to me."

But Moni never ceased singing and yodeling the whole summer long. For there was hardly another human being in the world as happy as he was up there with his goats. Often, he lay stretched out in his contentment on Pulpit Rock, gazing down into the sunny valley below. At such times, he couldn't help but think how he had sat all that time under the Rain Rock with the heavy burden on his heart. He remembered how all his happiness had been gone. So he would say over and over in his heart: "I know now what I will do, so that it will never happen again. I will do nothing that will prevent me from looking up gladly to heaven because this is right to the dear Lord."

But if it chanced that Moni became too long absorbed in his meditation, one or another of the goats would come along, gaze wonderingly at him and try to attract his attention by bleating. Sometimes when he was pondering these things, the goats had to bleat for awhile before he heard them. However, when Maggie came and called after him longingly, then he heard at once. He would leap to his feet immediately, for his affectionate little kid always remained Moni's dearest possession.

The Unforgiving Servant

Jesus Christ

Then Peter came to Jesus and said, "Lord, how often shall my brother sin against me, and I forgive him? Up to seven times?" Jesus said to him, "I do not say to you, up to seven times, but up to seventy times seven."

"Therefore the kingdom of heaven is like a certain king who wanted to settle accounts with his servants. And when he had begun to settle accounts, one was brought to him who owed him ten thousand talents. But as he was not able to pay, his master commanded that he be sold, with his wife and children and all that he had, and that payment be made.

The servant therefore fell down before him, saying, "Master, have patience with me, and I will pay you all." Then the master of that servant was moved with compassion, released him, and forgave him the debt.

But that servant went out and found one of his fellow servants who owed him a hundred denarii; and he laid hands on him and took him by the throat, saying, "Pay me what you owe!"

So his fellow servant fell down at his feet and begged him, saying, "Have patience with me, and I will pay you all." And he would not, but went and threw him into prison till he should pay the debt.

So when his fellow servants saw what had been done, they were very grieved, and came and told their master all that had been done. Then his master, after he had called him, said to him, "You wicked servant! I forgave you all that debt because you begged me. Should you not also have had compassion on your fellow servant, just as I had pity on you?" And his master was angry, and delivered him to the torturers until he should pay all that was due to him. So My heavenly Father also will do to you if each of you, from his heart, does not forgive his brother his trespasses."[3]

---

[3] Matt 18:21-35 (NKJV)

A Spark Neglected Burns The House

Leo Tolstoy

There once lived in a Russian village a peasant named Ivan Tarakan. He was comfortably off, in the prime of life, and the best worker in the village. He had three sons all able to work. The eldest was married and the second was about to marry. The third was a big lad who could mind the horses, and he was already beginning to plow. Ivan's wife was an able and thrifty woman, and they were fortunate in having a quiet, hard-working daughter-in-law. There was nothing to prevent Ivan and his family from living happily.

They had only one person to feed who was unable to work, and that was Ivan's old father. He suffered from asthma and had been lying ill on a bed for seven years. The bed was situated on the top of the brick oven in order to provide warmth for the elderly man. Ivan had all the material things he needed: three horses and a colt, a cow with a calf, and fifteen sheep. The women made all the clothing for the family, besides helping in the fields. And the men tilled the land. They always had grain enough of their own to last over beyond the next harvest, and they sold enough oats to pay their taxes and meet their other needs. So Ivan and his children might have lived quite comfortably had it not been for a feud between him and his next-door neighbor, Gabriel Petrov, the son of Viktor Kachko.

While old Viktor was still living and Ivan's father was still able to manage the household, the peasants lived as neighbors should. If the women of either house happened to need a pot or a tub, or the men needed a farm implement—or if a cart-wheel got broken and could not be mended at once—they used to send to the other house. Everyone helped each other in neighborly fashion. When a calf strayed into the neighbor's threshing-ground, they would simply drive it out. Rather than becoming angry, they would only say to their neighbor, "Oh, it would be good if you didn't let the calf stray again. Our grain is lying there on the threshing floor." In those days, no one thought of locking up the barns and outbuildings. No one hid things from one another, and no one dreamed of backbiting or grumbling at their neighbors.

That was in the days of the fathers. However, when the sons came to be at the head of the families, everything changed.

It all began over a trifle.

Ivan's daughter-in-law had a hen that began laying rather early in the season, and she started collecting its eggs. Every day she went to the cart shed, and she would find an egg in the cart. However, one day—frightened by the children—the hen flew across the fence into the neighbor's yard and laid its egg there. The woman had heard the hen cackling, but said to herself: "I have no time now. I must tidy up for Sunday. I'll fetch the egg later on."

In the evening she went to the cart, but she found no egg there. She went and asked her mother-in-law and brother-in-law if they had taken the egg. "No," they assured her. However, her youngest brother-in-law, Boris, said: "Your hen laid its egg in the neighbor's yard. It was there that she was cackling, and she flew back across the fence from there."

The woman went and looked at the hen. There she was on the perch with the other birds, her eyes just closing to go to sleep. The woman wished she could ask the hen about the egg, but of course she couldn't.

Then she went to the neighbor's, and Gabriel's mother came out to meet her.

"What do you want, young woman?"

"Why, Granny, you see, my hen flew across your fence this morning. Did she not lay an egg here?"

Gabriel's mother replied crossly, "We never saw anything of it. The Lord be thanked, our own hens started laying long ago. We collect our own eggs and have no need of other people's! And we don't go looking for eggs in other people's yards, young lady!"

The young woman was offended, and, in return, she said more than she should have. The older woman answered back even more rudely, and soon the women began shouting at each other. Ivan's wife, who had gone to fetch water, happened to pass by just then. Soon she joined in as well. Gabriel's wife rushed out, and began reproaching the young woman about various offenses that had really happened—and with other things that never had happened at all. Then a general uproar began, and everyone was shouting at once, trying to get out two words at a time (and not choice words either!).

"You're this!" and "You're that!" and "You're a thief!" and "You're a moron!" and "You're starving your old father-in-law to death!" and "You're a good-for-nothing!" and so on.

Someone shouted, "And you've made a hole in the sieve I lent you, you ungrateful oaf! And it's our yoke you're carrying your pails on, so just give our yoke back!"

Then they caught hold of the yoke and spilled the water. They snatched off one another's shawls and began fighting. Gabriel, returning from the fields, stopped and sided with his wife. Out rushed Ivan and his son and joined in with the rest. Ivan was a strong fellow, and he soon scattered the whole lot of them. He even pulled a handful of hair out of Gabriel's beard. People came to see what the matter was, and the fighters were separated only with great difficulty.

That was how it all began.

Gabriel wrapped the hair torn from his beard in a piece of paper, and he went to the District Court to call out the law against Ivan. "I didn't grow my beard for that idiot Ivan to pull it out!" he said. And his wife went bragging to the neighbors, saying they'd have Ivan condemned and sent to Siberia. And so the feud grew.

The old man, from where he lay on the top of the oven, tried from the very first to persuade the younger families to make peace, but they would not listen. He told them, "It's a stupid thing you're arguing about. You're acting like children, picking quarrels about such a paltry matter. Just think! The whole thing began about an *egg*. The children may have taken it. And, if so, so what? What's the value of one egg? God sends enough for all! And suppose your neighbor did say an unkind word. Set things right by showing her how to say a better one! If there *has* been a dispute, well, such things will happen. We're all sinners. But patch things up, and let there be an end of it! If you nurse your anger, it will only make things worse for all of you."

But the younger folk would not listen to the old man. They thought his words were mere senseless babbling. Ivan would not humble himself before his neighbor.

"I never pulled his beard," Ivan said. "He pulled the hair out himself. But his son has burst all the buttons on my shirt, and torn it. . . . Just look at it!"

And Ivan also went to law. Their quarrel went before the Justice of the Peace and then before the District Court. While all this was going on, the coupling-pin of Gabriel's cart disappeared. Gabriel's womenfolk accused Ivan's son of having taken it. They said: "We saw him in the night go past our window towards the cart. And a neighbor says he saw him at the pub, trying to sell the pin to the landlord."

So they went to court about that. And at home not a day passed without a quarrel or even a fight. The children, too, abused one another, having learned to do so from their elders. When the women happened to meet by the riverside—where they went to wash their clothes—their arms did not do as much wringing as their tongues did nagging. And every word was a bad one.

At first the peasants only *slandered* each other. But before long, they began in real earnest to snatch anything that lay handy. And soon the children followed their example. Life became harder and harder for them. Ivan Tarakan and Gabriel Petrov kept suing one another at the Village Assembly, at the District Court, and before the Justice of the Peace. It wasn't long before all the judges were tired of them. Sometimes Gabriel got Ivan fined or imprisoned. Then Ivan did the same to Gabriel. The more they spited each other, the angrier they grew.

They were like dogs that attack one another and get more and more furious the longer they fight. If someone strikes one dog from behind, it thinks it's the other dog biting him, and it gets still fiercer. It was the same with these peasants: they went to law and one or the other of them was fined or locked up. But that only made them angrier and angrier with each other. "Just you wait," they would say to each other, "and I'll make you pay for it." And so it went on for six years. Only the old man lying on the top of the oven kept telling them again and again: "Children, what are you doing? Stop all this paying back evil for evil. Keep to your work and don't bear malice towards one another. It will make life better for you. The more you bear malice, the worse it will be for all of you."

But they wouldn't listen to him.

In the seventh year of the feud, at a wedding, Ivan's daughter-in-law held Gabriel up to shame, accusing him of having been caught horse-stealing. Gabriel had been drinking, and he was unable to contain his anger. He gave the woman such a blow that she was laid up in bed for a week. What's more, she was pregnant at the time. Ivan was delighted. He went to the magistrate to lodge a complaint. "Now I'll get rid of my neighbor! This time he won't escape imprisonment or exile to Siberia." But Ivan's wish was not fulfilled. The magistrate dismissed the case. The woman was examined by a doctor, but she was up and about and showed no sign of any injury.

Ivan went next to the Justice of the Peace, but he referred the matter to the District Court. Ivan decided on a plan. He treated the clerk and the judge of the District Court to a gallon of vodka, and he got Gabriel condemned to be flogged. The sentence was read out to Gabriel by the clerk: "The Court decrees that the peasant Gabriel Petrov shall receive twenty lashes with a birch rod at the District Court."

Ivan heard the sentence read, and he looked at Gabriel to see how he would take it. Gabriel grew as pale as a sheet, and he turned round and went out into the hallway. Ivan followed him, intending to gloat over his victory. But in the hallway, he overheard Gabriel say, "Very well! He will have my back flogged, and that will make it burn. But something of his may burn worse than that!"

Hearing these words, Ivan at once went back into the Court, and said: "Upright judges! He threatens to set my house on fire! Listen! He said it in the presence of witnesses!'

Gabriel was recalled, and the judges asked him, "Is it true that you said this?"

"I haven't said anything. Flog me, since you have the power. It seems that I alone am to suffer—and all for being in the right. Meanwhile, he is allowed to do as he likes."

Gabriel wished to say something more, but his lips and his cheeks quivered, and he turned towards the wall. Even the officials were frightened by his looks. "He may well do some mischief to himself or to his neighbor," they thought.

Then the old Judge said: "Look here, my men. You'd better behave reasonably and make it up. Was it right of you, Gabriel, to strike a pregnant woman? It was lucky that things turned out all right. But think what might have happened! Was it right? You had better confess and beg his pardon, and he will forgive you. If so, we will alter the sentence."

The clerk heard these words, and remarked: "That's impossible under Statute 117. An agreement between the parties not having been arrived at, a decision of the Court has been pronounced and must be executed."

But the Judge would not listen to the clerk.

"Keep your tongue still, my friend," he said. "The first of all laws is to obey God, who loves peace." And the Judge began again to try to persuade the peasants, but he could not succeed. Gabriel would not listen to him.

"I shall be fifty next year," Gabriel said, "and have a married son, and have never been flogged in my life. And now that idiot Ivan has had me condemned to be flogged. And am I to go and ask his forgiveness? Never! I've suffered enough. But rest assured, Ivan shall have cause to remember me!"

Again Gabriel's voice quivered, and he could say no more. Instead, he turned and went out of the courthouse.

It was seven miles from the Court to the village, and it was getting late when Ivan reached home. He unharnessed his horse, put it up for the night, and entered his cottage. No one was there. The women had already gone to drive the cattle in, and the young fellows were not yet back from the fields. Ivan went in, sat down, and began thinking.

He remembered how Gabriel had listened to the sentence, and how pale he had become. He remembered how Gabriel had turned to the wall, and Ivan's heart grew heavy. He thought how he himself would feel if he were sentenced, and he pitied Gabriel. Then he heard his old father up on the oven cough, and saw him sit up, lower his legs, and scramble down. The old man dragged himself slowly to a chair and sat down. He was quite tired out with the exertion, and coughed a long time. Then, leaning against the table, he said: "Well, has he been condemned?"

"Yes, to twenty strokes with the rods," Ivan answered.

The old man shook his head.

"A bad thing," he said. "You are doing wrong, Ivan! Ah! It's a very bad thing—not for him so much as for you! So they'll flog him. But will that do *you* any good?"

"It'll teach him not to do it again," said Ivan.

"What is it he'll not do again? What has he done worse than you?"

"Why, think of the harm he has done me!" said Ivan. "He nearly killed my wife, and now he's threatening to burn us up. Am I to thank him for it?"

The old man sighed and said: "You move about the wide world, Ivan, while I have been lying on the oven all these years. So you think you see everything, and that I see nothing. Ah, lad! It's *you* that doesn't see. Hatred blinds you. Others' sins are before your eyes, but your own are behind your back."

"But he's acted badly!" Ivan retorted.

"What a thing to say! If he were the only one to act badly, how could strife exist? Is strife among men ever bred by one person alone? Strife is always between two. You see *his* badness, but not your own. If he were bad, but you were good, there would be no strife. Who pulled the hair out of his beard? Who ruined his haystack? Who dragged him to the law court? It was you!"

Ivan's father continued, "Yet you put it all on him! You live a bad life yourself. That's what is wrong! It's not the way I used to live, son, and it's not the way I taught you. Is that the way his old father and I used to live? How did we live? Why, as neighbors should! If he happened to run out of flour, one of the women would come over to our hut and say: "Uncle Taras, we need some flour."

"Go to the barn, dear," I'd say. "Take what you need."

"If he had no one to take his horses to pasture, I'd say, 'Go, Ivan, and look after his horses.' And if I was short of anything, I'd go to him. 'Uncle Viktor,' I'd say, 'I want so-and-so!' 'Take it, Uncle Taras!' That's how it was between us, and life was pleasant. But look at things now!"

"The other day," Ivan's father said, "a soldier was telling us about the fighting at Plevna between the Turks and the Russians. Why, the war between you is worse than at Plevna! Is that how Christians live? What a sin it is! You are a man and master of the house. It's you who will have to answer. What kind of example are you setting for the women and the children? To snarl and snap? Why, the other day your young son Boriska was swearing at our young neighbor Irena, calling her names. Yet, his mother only listened and laughed. Is that right? It is *you* who will have to answer. Think of your soul."

"Is this all as it should be?" Ivan's father asked. "You throw a word at your neighbor, and he gives you two in return. You give him a blow, and he give you two. No, lad! Christ, when He walked on earth, taught us fools something very different: If you receive an angry word from anyone, keep silent. His own conscience will accuse him. That is what our Lord taught. If you get a slap, turn the other cheek. Tell the other person, 'Here, beat me, if that's what I deserve!' And that man's own conscience will rebuke him. He will soften and will listen to you. That's the way He taught us, not to be proud! ...Ivan, why don't you speak? Isn't it as I say?"

Ivan remained silent.

The old man coughed, and only with difficulty was he able to clear his throat. He finally began again: "Do you think Christ taught us incorrectly? Why, it's all for our own good. Just think of your earthly life. Are you better off, or worse, since this feud began among you? Just count up what you've spent on all this law business. Think what's it all cost you to drive back and forth to town and have to pay for meals during your travels. You now have less than you did before. And why? All because of this folly—because of your pride.

"You ought to be plowing with your boys and sowing seeds for the next crop. But Gabriel carries you off to the judge. As a result, the plowing is not done in time, nor the sowing. As a result, you end up with a poor harvest. Why did the oats fail this year? When did you sow them? When you came back from town! And what did you gain? A burden for your own shoulders. Son, tend to your own business! Work with your boys in the field and at home. If someone offends you, forgive him, as God wishes you to. Then life will be pleasant, and your heart will always be light."

Ivan still remained silent.

"Ivan, my son, hear your old father! Go and harness the pony, and go at once to the government office. Put an end to all this affair there. And in the morning, go and patch things up with Gabriel in God's name. In fact, invite him to your house for tomorrow's holiday. Have tea and bread ready and put an end to this wicked business, so that there'll be no more of it in the future. And tell the women and children to do the same."

Ivan sighed, and thought, "What he says is true," and his heart grew lighter. Only he didn't know quite how to begin putting matters right.

But the old man spoke again, as if he had guessed what was in Ivan's mind: "Go, Ivan, don't put it off! Put out the fire before it spreads, or it will be too late."

Ivan's father was going to say more, but before he could do so the women came in, chattering like magpies. The news that Gabriel was sentenced to be flogged—and of his threat to set fire to the house—had already reached them. They had heard all about it and added to it something of their own. And once again, out in the pasture, they had a quarrel with the women of Gabriel's household. They began telling how Gabriel's daughter-in-law threatened a fresh legal action. She said that Gabriel had got the examining magistrate on his side, who would now turn the whole affair upside down.

They also said that the schoolmaster was writing out another petition about Ivan—to the Czar himself this time. They were told that everything would be in the petition—all about the coupling-pin and the kitchen garden. Gabriel's family was gloating that half of Ivan's homestead would soon be theirs.

Ivan heard what they were saying, and his heart grew cold again, and he gave up the thought of making peace with Gabriel.

In a farmstead there is always plenty for the master to do. Ivan did not stop to talk to the women but went out to the threshing-floor and then to the barn. By the time he had tidied up the barn, the sun had set and the young fellows had returned from the field. They had been plowing the field with two horses for the winter crops. Ivan met them, asked them how their work had gone, and helped them to put all the implements in their places. He noticed that one of the horse's collars was torn, and he set the collar aside to be mended. He was then going to put away some stakes in the barn, but by now it had grown quite dark. Therefore, he decided to leave them where they were until the next day. Finally, he gave the cattle their food.

"Now," he thought, "I'll have my supper and then go to bed." He took the horse collar and entered the hut. By this time, he had forgotten about Gabriel and about what his elderly father had been saying to him. But just as he took hold of the door handle to enter the passage, he heard his neighbor on the other side of the fence cursing somebody in a hoarse voice:

"What is he good for?" Gabriel was saying. "He's only fit to be killed!" At these words, all of Ivan's former bitterness towards his neighbor was reawakened. He stood listening while Gabriel ranted. When Gabriel finally stopped, Ivan went into his hut.

There was a light inside. His daughter-in-law sat spinning, and his wife was getting supper ready. His eldest son was making straps for bark shoes, his second-oldest sat near the table with a book, and Boris (his youngest) was getting ready to go out to pasture the horses for the night. Everything in the hut would have been pleasant and bright, but for the tension with the neighbors.

Ivan entered the room, sullen and cross. He shoved the cat down from the bench, and he scolded the women for putting the slop pail in the wrong place. Frowning and feeling despondent, he sat down to mend the horse collar. Gabriel's words kept ringing in his ears: his threat of petitioning the Czar and what he had just been shouting in a hoarse voice about someone who was "only fit to be killed."

Ivan's wife gave Boris his supper first. Having eaten it, Boris put on an old sheepskin coat, tied a sash round his waist, took some bread with him, and went out to the horses. His oldest brother was going to see him off, but Ivan himself rose instead, and went out onto the porch. It had grown quite dark outside, clouds had gathered, and the wind had risen. Ivan went down the steps, helped his boy to mount, started the foal after him, and stood listening while Boris rode down to the village, where he was joined by other lads with their horses. Ivan waited until they were all out of sight. As he stood there by the gate, he could not get Gabriel's words out of his head: "Mind that something of yours does not burn worse!"

"He is desperate," thought Ivan. "Everything is dry, and it's windy weather besides. He'll come up at the back somewhere, set fire to something, and be off. He'll burn the place and escape scot free, the villain! However, if someone could catch him in the act, he'd not get off then!"

The thought fixed itself so firmly in Ivan's mind that he did not go up the steps but went out into the street and around the corner. "I'll just walk around the buildings," he said to himself. "After all, who can tell what he might do?" Stepping softly, Ivan went outside the gate. As soon as he reached the corner, he looked around along the fence. He thought he saw something suddenly move at the opposite corner—as if someone had come out and disappeared again. Ivan stopped, and he stood quietly, listening and looking. Everything was still. Only the leaves of the willows fluttered in the wind, and the straws of the thatch rustled. When Ivan's eyes had grown used to the darkness, he could see the far corner, and a plough that lay there. He gazed a while but saw no one.

"I suppose I was mistaken," thought Ivan. "But I'll still go around all the buildings and check." Ivan went stealthily along by the shed. He stepped so softly in his bark shoes that he couldn't hear even his own footsteps. As he reached the far corner, something seemed to flare up for a moment near the plough and then vanish again. Ivan felt as if he had been struck to the heart, and he immediately stopped. Hardly had he stopped when something flared up more brightly in the same place. Ivan now could clearly see a man with a cap on his head, crouching down with his back towards him. He was lighting a bunch of straw he held in his hand. Ivan's heart fluttered within him like a bird. Straining every nerve, he approached with great strides, hardly feeling his legs under him. "Ah," thought Ivan, "now he won't escape! I'll catch him in the act!"

Ivan was still some distance off, when suddenly he saw a bright light, but not in the same place as before, and not a small flame. The thatch had flared up at the eaves, and the flames were reaching up to the roof. Standing beneath it all, Gabriel's whole figure was clearly visible.

Like a hawk swooping down on a lark, Ivan rushed at Gabriel. "Now I'll have him. He won't escape me!" thought Ivan. But Gabriel heard his steps, and glancing round, he scuttled away past the barn like a hare.

"You won't escape!" shouted Ivan, darting after him.

Just as he was about to seize the culprit, Gabriel dodged him. Ivan managed only to catch the skirt of Gabriel's coat. It tore right off, and Ivan fell down. He jumped back to his feet, and ran after Gabriel shouting, "Help! Seize him! Thief! Murder!" Meanwhile Gabriel had reached his own gate. There Ivan overtook him and was about to seize him, when something struck Ivan a stunning blow, as though a stone had hit his temple. It was Gabriel who, seizing an oak wedge that lay near the gate, had struck out with all his might.

Ivan was stunned. Stars flew before his eyes. Then all grew dark. When Ivan came to his senses, Gabriel was no longer there. It was as light as day, and from the side where his homestead was situated, something roared and crackled like an engine at work. Ivan turned around and saw that his back shed was all ablaze and that the side shed had also caught fire. Flames and smoke and bits of burning straw were being driven towards his hut.

"What has happened?" cried Ivan, lifting his arms and striking his thighs. "Why, all I had to do was just to snatch the burning straw out from under the eaves and trample on it!" He tried to shout, but his breath failed him. His voice was gone. He wanted to run, but his legs wouldn't obey him. Instead, they got in each other's way. Ivan moved slowly, but he again staggered and again his breath failed him. He stood still until he had regained his breath, and he then went on. Before he had reached the back shed to stop the fire, the side shed was also all ablaze.

Soon the corner of the hut and the covered gateway had caught fire as well. The flames were leaping out of the hut, and it was impossible to get into the yard. A large crowd had collected, but nothing could be done. The neighbors were carrying their belongings out of their own houses, and driving the cattle out of their own sheds. After Ivan's house, Gabriel's house also caught fire. Then, the wind picked up, the flames spread to the other side of the street, and half the village was burned down.

At Ivan's house, they barely managed to save his old father. And the family escaped in what they had on. Everything else was lost, except for the horses that had been driven out to pasture for the night. All the cattle, the hens on their perches, the carts, ploughs, and harrows, the women's trunks with their clothes, and the grain in the granaries—all were burned up!

At Gabriel's place, the cattle were driven out, and only a few things were saved from his house.

The fire lasted all night. Ivan stood in front of his homestead and kept repeating, "What has happened? One needed only to have pulled it out and trampled on it!" But when the roof fell in, Ivan rushed into the burning place. Seizing a charred beam, he tried to drag it out. The women saw him and called him back. Ivan managed to pull out the beam, and he was going in again for another when he lost his footing and fell among the flames.

Quickly his son made his way in after Ivan and dragged him out. Ivan had singed his hair and beard. He had burned his clothes and scorched his hands, but he felt nothing. "His grief has stupefied him," the people said. The fire was burning itself out, but Ivan still stood repeating: "What has happened? One needed only to have pulled it out!'

In the morning the village elder's son came to fetch Ivan. "Ivan," he called. "Your father is dying! He has sent for you to say good-bye."

Ivan had forgotten about his father, and didn't understand what was being said to him.

"Whose father?" he said. "Whom has he sent for?"

"He sent for you, to say good-bye. He is dying in our cottage! Come along, Ivan," the elder's son urged, pulling him by the arm. Ivan followed the lad.

When Ivan's father was being carried out of the hut, some burning straw had fallen on to him and burned him. He had been taken to the village elder's house in the farther part of the village, which the fire did not reach.

When Ivan came to his father, there was only the elder's wife in the hut, besides some little children on the top of the oven. All the rest were still at the fire.

The old man, who was lying on a bench, kept turning his eyes towards the door. When his son entered, he moved a little. The old woman went up to him and told him that his son had come. He asked to have him brought nearer. Ivan came closer.

"What did I tell you, Ivan?" began the old man. "Who has burned down the village?"

"It was he, father!" Ivan answered. "I caught him in the act. I saw him shove the firebrand into the thatch. I might have pulled away the burning straw and stamped it out, and then nothing would have happened."

"Ivan," said the old man, "I am dying, and you in your turn will have to face death. Whose is the sin?"

Ivan gazed at his father in silence, unable to utter a word.

"Now, before God, say whose sin it is. What did I tell you?"

Only then did Ivan come to his senses, and he then understood it all. He sniffed and said, "Mine, father!" And he fell on his knees before his father, saying, "Forgive me, father. I am guilty before you and before God."

The old man moved his hands and tried to lift his right hand to trace the sign of the cross, but he couldn't do it and so stopped.

"Praise the Lord! Praise the Lord!" he said, and again he turned his eyes towards his son.

"Ivan! I say, Ivan!"

"What, father?"

"What must you do now?"

Ivan was weeping.

"I don't know how we are to live now, father!" he said.

The old man closed his eyes, moved his lips as if to gather strength, and opening his eyes again, he said: "You'll manage. If you obey God's will, you'll manage!" He paused, then smiled, and said: "Mind what I say, Ivan! Don't tell anyone who started the fire! Cover another man's sin. As Jesus said, 'If you forgive men their trespasses, your heavenly Father will also forgive you.'" And the old man took the nearby candle in both hands and, folding them on his breast, sighed, stretched out, and died.

Ivan wept bitterly. He had lost his home, his belongings, and now his father, simply because he had refused to forgive. He went outside and walked through a nearby field. As he walked, he cried and prayed to God for forgiveness. He saw how wrong he had been through all of the turmoil, and he repented deeply. Finally, before God, he unconditionally forgave Gabriel and his family.

Ivan never said anything against Gabriel, and no one knew what had caused the fire.

Gabriel wondered why Ivan had not told anybody. So after several months, he approached Ivan and asked him why he had not said anything to anyone.

"Because I was as much at fault as you were. And I forgave you completely the day my father died. So please don't be afraid. I will never tell anyone how the fire started." Ivan hesitated for a moment and then added, "Can we be friends again?"

Gabriel was speechless for a moment. He then began to cry and then warmly embraced Ivan. "No, I was the one at fault, not you," he said. "I'm so sorry for the wrong I have done and the poor example I set for my family and others." Gabriel then smiled and said, "Yes, we can be friends again!" He then kissed Ivan on each cheek.

Now that the men had forgiven each other, their families forgave each other also. While rebuilding their huts, both families lived in one house. Even when the village was rebuilt and they might have moved further apart, Ivan and Gabriel built their homes next to each other and remained neighbors as before. In fact, they lived as good neighbors should.

Ivan Tarakan remembered his old father's command to obey God's law and to quench a fire at the first spark. Now, if anyone does him an injury, he does not take revenge. Instead, he works to set matters right again. If anyone speaks a bad word to him, he doesn't give a worse in return. Rather, he tries to teach the other person not to use evil words. And so he teaches his womenfolk and children. Yes, Ivan Tarakan is on his feet again, and he now lives better even than he did before—before both man and God.

Androcles and the Lion

Traditional

In Rome there was once a poor Christian slave whose name was Androcles. His master was a cruel man, and when he discovered that Androcles was a Christian, he threatened to put him to death. So Androcles ran away one night.

He hid himself in a wild wood for many days. But there was no food to be found, and he grew so weak and sick that he thought he would die. So one day he crept into a cave and lay down. Soon he was fast asleep.

However, before long, a great noise awoke him. A lion had come into the cave and was roaring loudly. Androcles was very much afraid, for he felt sure that the beast would kill him. He silently prayed to God for deliverance. When he finished praying, Androcles realized that the lion was not ferocious. Instead, he limped as though his foot hurt him.

With God's strength, Androcles grew so bold that he took hold of the lion's lame paw to see what the matter was. The lion stood quite still and even rubbed his head against the man's shoulder. He seemed to be saying, "I know that you will help me."

Androcles lifted the lion's paw from the ground, and saw that it had a long, sharp thorn in it. This is what hurt the lion so much. Androcles took the end of the thorn in his fingers, and he then gave a strong, quick pull. Out the thorn came! The lion was full of joy. He jumped about like a dog, and licked the hands and feet of his new friend.

Androcles thanked God for this miracle. He was not at all afraid after this. In fact, when night came, he and the lion lay down and slept side by side. For a long time, the lion brought food to Androcles every day, and the two became such good friends that Androcles found his new life with the lion a very happy one.

However, one day some soldiers passed through the woods, looking for Androcles. Peering into the cave with torches, they soon found Androcles and bound him with chains. Mocking and threatening him, they brusquely dragged him back to Rome.

Many years before, the Roman emperor had outlawed Christianity. Any Christian who was caught and who refused to renounce Christ was sent to the arena to be torn apart by a hungry lion. Although he was savagely beaten, Androcles refused to deny Christ. So he was locked in prison, and a date was set for him to be thrown to a lion. Several lions were kept in cages below the ground floor of the arena. They were fed very little so that they would be that much more fierce and hungry.

When the appointed day came, thousands of people crowded in the arena to see the sport. In those days, Romans went to the arena for amusement, much the same way that Americans today got to circuses or ball games.

The door to the arena floor opened, and poor Androcles was brought in. He was almost dead with fear, for he could hear the roar of the lions in their cages.. He looked out at the crowd and saw that there was no pity in the thousands of faces around him. He knelt and prayed to God for His deliverance and for the strength to remain faithful if God chose not to deliver him.

Then one of the lion cages was raised to the surface through a trap door, and a hungry lion rushed out of the cage. At first, the lion slowly looked around the arena to get his bearings. Then spying a lone man kneeling in one corner, he quickly charged at him. As the lion came close, Androcles looked up—expecting his death. He immediately let out a great cry. But it was not a cry of fear, but a cry of joy. For he realized that the lion was his old friend, the lion of the cave.

The people, who had expected to see the man torn apart by the lion, were filled with wonder. They were even more amazed when they saw Androcles put his arms around the lion's neck. And they were in utter disbelief when they saw the lion lie down at Androcles' feet and lick him lovingly. In fact, the great beast rubbed his head against the slave's face as though he wanted to be petted. The crowd could not understand what it all meant, but they realized that they were witnessing a miracle.

After a while, the tribune motioned Androcles to approach his chair in the stands. He then asked Androcles to explain what had happened. Androcles stood before the tribunal without fear, with the lion at his side. He told the tribunal about the great God he served, and how his God had now delivered him twice—once in the cave and now in the arena.

"I am a man," he said, "but my master has never treated me as a brother, as a fellow man. Yet, this poor lion has been kind to me, and we love each other as brothers."

The tribune was so moved by the poor slave's testimony that he declared: "Live and be free!" Soon the people in the stands also cried out, "Live and be free!"

Others cried, "Let the lion go free too! Give both of them their liberty!"

And so Androcles was set free, and the lion was given to him for his own. And they lived together for many years.

The War Prayer

Mark Twain

It was a time of great exulting and excitement. The country was up in arms, and the war was on. In every breast burned the holy fire of patriotism. The drums were beating, the bands playing, the toy pistols popping, and bunches of firecrackers hissing and sputtering. On every hand and far down the receding and fading spread of roofs and balconies, a fluttering wilderness of flags flashed in the sun. Every day the young volunteers marched down the wide avenue cheerful and fine in their new uniforms. The proud fathers, mothers, sisters and sweethearts cheered them with voices choked with happy emotion as they marched by.

Every night the packed throngs listened breathlessly to patriot oratory that stirred the deepest depths of their hearts. They interrupted these glowing speeches every few minutes with cyclones of applause. All the while, tears were running down their cheeks. In the churches, the pastors preached devotion to flag and country. With outpourings of fervid eloquence that moved every listener, the preachers invoked the God of Battles, beseeching His aid in their good cause.

It was indeed a joyous and congenial time. Those few voices that ventured to disapprove of the war and to cast doubt upon its righteousness quickly got such a stern and angry warning that for their personal safety they quickly shrank out of sight and offended the public no more.

Sunday morning came, and the next day the battalions would leave for the front. The church was filled. The volunteers were all there, their young faces alight with military dreams: visions of the stern advance, the gathering momentum, the rushing charge, the flashing sabers, the flight of the foe, the tumult, the enveloping smoke, the fierce pursuit, and the enemy's quick surrender! After that, there would be the glorious homecoming from the war. They would return as bronzed heroes, welcomed, adored, submerged in golden seas of glory!

With the volunteers sat their dear ones, proud, happy, and envied by the neighbors and friends who had no sons and brothers to send forth to the field of honor—there to win victory for the flag, or failing, die the noblest of noble deaths. The service proceeded. A war chapter from the Old Testament was read. The first prayer was said. It was followed by an organ burst that shook the building. And with one impulse, the congregation rose, with glowing eyes and beating hearts, and poured out that tremendous invocation:

"God the all-terrible! Thou who ordains, thunder as thy clarion and lightning as thy sword!"

The short invocation was followed by the "long" prayer. No one could remember the likes of it for passionate pleading and moving, beautiful language. The burden of its supplication was that the ever-merciful and benign Father of us all would watch over our noble young soldiers, and aid, comfort, and encourage them in their patriotic work. The pastor prayed for God to bless them, shield them in the day of battle and the hour of peril, bear them in His mighty hand, and make them strong, confident, and invincible in the bloody onset. He prayed that God would help them to crush the foe and to grant to them and to their flag and country imperishable honor and glory.

Suddenly an aged stranger entered the church and moved with slow and noiseless steps up the main aisle. His eyes were fixed upon the minister as he walked. His long body was clothed in a robe that reached to his feet. He wore no hat, and his white hair descended like a frothy waterfall to his shoulders. His rough face was unnaturally pale, pale even to the point of ghastliness. With all the eyes of the congregation following his path and wondering who he was, he made his silent way to the front. Without pausing, he ascended to the preacher's side and stood there, waiting. With shut eyelids, the preacher was unconscious of his presence. So he continued his moving prayer. He at last finished it with words uttered in fervent appeal: "Bless our arms and grant us victory, O Lord our God, Father and Protector of our land and flag!"

The stranger touched the minister's arm and motioned him to step aside—which the startled minister did. The stranger then took the minister's place in the pulpit. For a few moments, he surveyed the spellbound audience with solemn eyes, in which burned an uncanny light. Finally, in a deep voice he said:

"I come from the Throne—bearing a message from Almighty God!" The words struck the congregation with a shock. However, if the stranger perceived their shock, he paid it no attention.

He continued, "God has heard the prayer of His servant, your shepherd, and will grant it if such is still your desire after I, His messenger, shall have explained to you its import—that is to say, its full significance. For it is like many other prayers of men, in that it asks for more than he who utters it is aware of—unless he pauses and thinks about it.

"God's servant and yours has prayed his prayer. Has he paused and taken thought of its full significance? Is it one prayer? No, it is actually two—one uttered, the other not. Both have reached the ear of Him Who hears all supplications—both the spoken and the unspoken. Ponder this, and keep it in mind. If you would beseech a blessing upon yourself, beware! For without intent, you may be invoking a curse upon your neighbor at the same time. For example, you may pray for the blessing of rain upon your crop that needs it. However, by that act you are possibly praying for a curse upon some neighbor's crop that may not need rain and will be ruined by it.

"You have heard your minister's prayer—the uttered part of it. I am commissioned by God to put into words the other part of it. I'm referring to the part which the pastor (and also you in your hearts) fervently prayed for silently. And perhaps ignorantly and unthinkingly as well. I hope that it was so! You heard these words: 'Grant us victory, O Lord our God!' That is sufficient. The *whole* of the uttered prayer is summed up in those weighty words. Elaborations were not necessary. When you have prayed for victory you have prayed for many unmentioned results which follow victory. Things that *must* follow it. Things that cannot help but follow it. Upon the listening spirit of God the Father fell also the unspoken part of the prayer. He commands me to put it into words. Listen to the unspoken part of your prayer:

"O Lord our Father, our young patriots, idols of our hearts, go forth to battle. Be Thou near them! *We* also go forth with them in spirit from the sweet peace of our beloved firesides to smite the foe. O Lord our God, help us to rip their soldiers to bloody shreds with our shells. Help us to cover their smiling fields with the pale forms of their dead patriots. Help us to drown the thunder of the guns with the shrieks of their wounded, writhing in pain. Help us to lay waste their humble homes with hurricanes of fire.

"Help us to wring the hearts of their unoffending widows with never-ending grief. Help us to turn their widows out roofless with their little children, to helplessly wander the wastes of their desolated land in rags, hunger and thirst. Help us to make them the sports of the searing heat of summer and the icy winds of winter. Make these widows—broken in spirit and worn with travail—implore Thee for the refuge of the grave. But deny it to them. We pray these things for our sakes, we who adore Thee. Please Lord, blast their hopes, blight their lives, protract their bitter pilgrimage, make heavy their steps, water their way with tears, stain the white snow with the blood of their wounded feet! We ask it, in the spirit of love, of Him Who is the Source of Love, and Who is the ever faithful refuge and friend of all who are sorely afflicted and seek His aid with humble and contrite hearts. Amen."

The strange messenger paused as he looked out at the congregation, looking deeply into their eyes. He then spoke with a grave and deliberate tone: "Yes, you have prayed it. If you still desire it, speak! The messenger of the Most High waits for your answer."

Sadly, however, the people dismissed the old man as a lunatic. For what he said made absolutely no sense to them.

The Good Samaritan

Jesus Christ

A teacher of the Law asked Jesus, "Who is my neighbor?" Then Jesus answered and said:

A certain man went down from Jerusalem to Jericho, and fell among thieves, who stripped him of his clothing, wounded him, and departed, leaving him half dead. Now by chance a certain priest came down that road. And when he saw him, he passed by on the other side. Likewise a Levite, when he arrived at the place, came and looked, and passed by on the other side.

But a certain Samaritan, as he journeyed, came where the wounded man was. And when he saw him, he had compassion. So he went to him and bandaged his wounds, pouring on oil and wine. And he set him on his own animal, brought him to an inn, and took care of him.

On the next day, when he departed, he took out two denarii, gave them to the innkeeper, and said to him, "Take care of him. And whatever more you spend, when I come again, I will repay you."

Jesus then asked the teacher, "So which of these three do you think was neighbor to him who fell among the thieves?"

And the teacher replied, "He who showed mercy on him."

Then Jesus said to him, "Go and do likewise."[4]

[4] Luke 10:30-37 (NKJV)

Where Love Is, God Is

Leo Tolstoy

In a little town in Russia there lived a cobbler named Martin. He had a tiny room in a basement, the one window of which looked out onto the street. Through it he could see only the feet of those who passed by, but Martin recognized the people by their boots. He had lived long in the place and had many acquaintances.

There was hardly a pair of boots in the neighborhood that had not been once or twice through his hands. As a result, he often saw his own handiwork through the window. Some he had re-soled, some patched, some stitched up, and to some he had even put fresh uppers. He had plenty of work, for he labored hard, used good material, did not charge too much, and could be relied on. If he could finish a job by the day requested, he undertook it. If not, he told the truth and gave no false promises. So he was well known and never short of work.

Martin had always been an honest man, but in his old age he began to think even more about his soul and to draw nearer to God.

From that time on, Martin's whole life changed. His life became peaceful and joyful. He sat down to his work in the morning, and when he had finished his day's work he took the lamp down from the wall, stood it on the table, fetched his Bible from the shelf, opened it, and sat down to read. The more he read, the better he understood, and the clearer and happier he felt in his mind.

It happened once that Martin sat up late, absorbed in his reading. He was reading Luke's Gospel, and in the sixth chapter he came upon these verses:

> "To him that smites you on the one cheek, offer also the other. And from him that takes away your cloak, do not withhold your coat either. Give to every man that asks of you. And of him that takes away your goods, do not ask for them back. And as you want men to do to you, do likewise to them."

He thought about this, and was about to go to bed, but he didn't want to put down his reading. So he went on reading the seventh chapter of Luke—about the centurion, the widow's son, and the answer to John's disciples. Eventually, he came to the part where a rich Pharisee invited the Lord to his house. And he read about the woman who—although a sinner—anointed His feet and washed them with her tears, and how He justified her. Coming to the forty-fourth verse, he read:

> And turning to the woman, he said unto Simon, "See this woman? I entered into your house, and you gave me no water for my feet. But she has washed my feet with her tears and wiped them with her hair. You gave me no kiss, but she, since the time I came in, has not ceased to kiss my feet. You did not anoint my head with oil, but she has anointed my feet with ointment."

He read these verses and thought: "He gave no water for his feet, he gave no kiss, his head with oil he did not anoint...." And then he took off his spectacles once more, laid them on his book, and pondered what he had read.

"He must have been like me, that Pharisee. He too thought only of himself—how to get a cup of tea, how to keep warm and comfortable, but never a thought for his guest. He took care of himself, but for his guest he cared nothing at all. Yet who was the guest? The Lord Himself! If he came to me, would I behave like that?"

Then Martin laid his head upon both his arms and—before he was aware of it—he fell asleep.

"Martin!" He suddenly heard a voice, as if someone had spoken right into his ear.

He was startled from his sleep. "Who's there?"he asked.

He turned around and looked at the door; no one was there. He called again. Then he heard quite distinctly: "Martin, Martin! Look out into the street tomorrow, for I shall come."

Martin roused himself, rose from his chair and rubbed his eyes. But he didn't know whether he had heard these words in a dream or while he was awake. He put out the lamp and lay down to sleep again.

The next morning he rose before daylight, and after praying, he lit the fire and prepared his cabbage soup and buckwheat porridge. Then he lit the kettle, put on his apron, and sat down by the window to his work. Actually, this day, he spent more time looking out his window than he did working. And whenever anyone passed by the window in unfamiliar boots, he would stoop down and look up, so he could see not only the feet but the face of the passerby as well.

A house servant passed by in new felt boots, then a water-carrier. Before long, an old man came near the window, with a shovel in his hand. Martin knew him by his boots, which were shabby old boots, made of felt and leather. The old man was called Ivan. A neighboring tradesman kept him in his house for charity, and his duty was to help the house servant. The old man began to clear away the snow in front of Martin's window. Martin glanced at him and then went on with his work.

After he had made a dozen stitches, Martin felt drawn to look out of the window again. He saw that Ivan had laid his spade against the wall and was either resting or trying to get warm. The man was old and broken down. It was evident that he didn't have enough strength to clear away the snow.

"What if I called him in and gave him some tea?" thought Martin. "The kettle is just now boiling."

He stuck his awl in its place and rose from his seat. Putting the kettle on the table, he made tea. Then he tapped on the window with his fingers. Ivan turned and came to the window. Martin beckoned to him to come in, and he himself went to open the door.

"Come in," Martin said, "and warm yourself a bit. I'm sure you must be cold."

"May God bless you!" Ivan answered. "My bones do ache, to be sure."

Ivan came in, shaking off the snow. And lest he should leave marks on the floor, he began wiping his feet. But as he did so he tottered and nearly fell.

"Don't trouble to wipe your feet," Martin said. "I'll wipe up the floor—it's all in the day's work. Come, friend, sit down and have some tea."

Filling two cups, Martin passed one cup to his visitor. Then, raising his own cup to his lips, Martin began to blow on it. Meanwhile, Ivan emptied his cup and—turning it upside down—he put the remains of his piece of sugar on the top. He began to express his thanks, but it was plain that he would be glad for some more.

"Have another cup," Martin said, refilling his visitor's cup and his own. But while he drank his tea, Martin kept looking out into the street.

"Are you expecting anyone?" Ivan asked.

"Am I expecting anyone? Well, now, I'm ashamed to tell you. It isn't that I really expect anyone, but I heard something last night that I can't get out of my mind. Whether it was a vision, or only a dream, I can't tell you. You see, friend, last night I was reading the Gospel about Christ the Lord—how He suffered and how He walked on earth. You have heard tell of it, I dare say."

"I have heard tell of it," answered Ivan. "But I'm an ignorant man and not able to read."

"Well, you see, I was reading how He walked on earth. I came to that part, you know, where He went to a Pharisee who did not receive Him well. Well, friend, as I read about it, I thought how that man did not receive Christ the Lord with proper honor.

Suppose such a thing could happen to such a man as myself? I thought, what would I not do to receive him! But that man gave him no reception at all.

"Well, friend, as I was thinking of this, I began to doze, and as I dozed I heard someone call me by name. I got up, and thought I heard someone whispering, 'Expect me. I will come tomorrow.' This happened twice. And to tell you the truth, it made such an impression on my mind that, although I'm a bit embarrassed, I keep on expecting Him, the dear Lord!"

Ivan shook his head in silence, finished his cup, and laid it on its side. However, Martin stood it up again and refilled it for him.

"Thank you, Martin," Ivan said. "You have given me food and comfort both for my soul and body."

"You're very welcome. Come again another time. I'm glad to have a guest," Martin said.

Ivan went away, and Martin poured out the last of the tea and drank it up. Then he put away the tea and kettle and sat down to his work, stitching the back seam of a boot. And as he stitched, he kept looking out of the window, and thinking about what he had read in the Bible. And his head was full of Christ's sayings.

Two soldiers went by: one in government boots the other in boots of his own. Then came the master of a neighboring house, in shining galoshes. Next came a baker carrying a basket. All these passed on. Then a woman came up in woolen stockings and peasant-made shoes. She passed the window, but stopped by the wall. Martin glanced up at her through the window.

He saw that she was a stranger, poorly dressed, and with a baby in her arms. She stood by the wall with her back to the wind, trying to wrap the baby up—even though she had hardly anything to wrap it in. The woman was wearing only summer clothes, and even they were shabby and worn. Through the window, Martin heard the baby crying. The woman was trying to soothe it, but she was unable to do so. Martin rose, and going out the door and up the steps, he called to her. "My dear woman, I say, my dear woman!"

The woman heard and turned around.

"Why do you stand out there with the baby in the cold? Come inside. You can wrap him up better in a warm place. Come this way!"

The woman was surprised to see an old man in an apron, with spectacles on his nose, calling to her, but she followed him in. They went down the steps, entered the little room, and the old man led her to the bed.

"There, sit down, my dear, near the stove. Warm yourself and nurse the baby."

"I can't seem to produce any milk for my baby. I've eaten nothing myself since early morning," the woman said. Nevertheless, she still tried to nurse her baby.

Martin shook his head. He brought out a bowl and some bread. Then he opened the oven door and poured some cabbage soup into the bowl. He took out the porridge pot also, but the porridge was not yet ready, so he spread a cloth on the table and served only the soup and bread.

"Sit down and eat, my dear, and I'll mind the baby. Why, bless me, I've had children of my own. I know how to manage them."

The woman prayed, and sitting down at the table she began to eat. Meanwhile, Martin put the baby on the bed and sat down by it.

Martin sighed. "Haven't you any warmer clothing?" he asked.

"How could I get warm clothing?" she said. "Why, I pawned my last shawl for six pennies yesterday."

Then the woman came and took the child, and Martin got up. He went and looked among some things that were hanging on the wall, and he brought back an old cloak.

"Here," he said, "though it's a worn-out old thing, it will suffice to wrap him up in."

The woman looked at the cloak, then at the old man, and taking it, burst into tears. Martin turned away, and groping under the bed brought out a small trunk. He fumbled about in it, and again sat down opposite the woman. And the woman said, "The Lord bless you, friend."

"Take this for the sake of Christ," Martin said, and he gave her six pennies to get her shawl out of pawn. The woman looked to heaven, and Martin did the same, and then he escorted her out.

After a while, Martin saw an apple woman stop just in front of his window. On her back, she had a sack full of wood chips, which she was taking home.

No doubt she had gathered them at someplace where building was going on.

The sack evidently hurt her, and she wanted to shift it from one shoulder to the other. Accordingly, she put the sack down on the footpath. Then, placing her basket on a post, she began to shake down the wood chips in the sack.

While she was doing this, a boy in a tattered cap ran up, snatched an apple out of her basket, and tried to slip away. But the old woman noticed it. And turning suddenly, she caught the boy by his sleeve. He began to struggle, trying to free himself, but the old woman held on with both hands. Eventually, she knocked his cap off his head, and seized hold of his hair.

The boy screamed and the old woman scolded. Martin dropped his awl—not waiting to stick it in its place—and rushed out of the door. Stumbling up the steps and dropping his spectacles in his hurry, he ran out into the street. The old woman was pulling the boy's hair, scolding him, and threatening to take him to the police. The lad was struggling and protesting, saying, "I did not take it. What are you beating me for? Let me go!"

Martin separated them. He took the boy by the hand and said, "Let him go, Grandmother. Forgive him for the sake of Christ."

"I'll teach him a lesson, so that he won't forget it for a year! I'll take the rascal to the police!"

Martin began entreating the old woman. "Let him go, Grandmother. He won't do it again."

The old woman let go, and the boy wished to run away, but Martin stopped him.

"Ask the Grandmother's forgiveness!" he said. "And don't do it another time. I saw you take the apple."

The boy began to cry and to beg forgiveness.

"That's right. And now here's an apple for you," Martin said, taking an apple from the basket and giving it to the boy. He told the old woman, "I will pay you, Grandmother."

"You will spoil them that way, the young rascals," snapped the old woman. "He ought to be whipped so that he should remember it for a week."

"Oh, Grandmother, Grandmother," Martin said, "That's *our* way, but it is not God's way. If he should be whipped for stealing an apple, what should be done to the rest of us for our sins?"

The old woman was silent.

And then Martin told her the parable of the king who forgave his servant a large debt, and how the servant went out and seized his debtor by the throat. The old woman listened to it all. The boy, too, stood by and listened.

"God asks us to forgive," Martin said, "or else we shall not be forgiven. We must forgive everyone—and a thoughtless youngster most of all."

The old woman nodded her head and sighed.

"It's true enough," she said, "but they are getting terribly spoiled."

"Then we old ones must show them better ways," Martin replied.

"That's just what I say," said the old woman. "I have had seven of them myself, and only one daughter is left."

And the old woman began to tell how and where she was living with her daughter, and how many grandchildren she had. "Nowadays," she said, "I have but little strength left. Yet I work hard for the sake of my grandchildren—and nice children they are, too. No one comes out to meet me but the grandchildren. Little Annie, now, won't leave me for anyone. It's 'Grandmother, dear Grandmother, darling Grandmother.'"

And the old woman completely softened her countenance at the thought.

"Of course, it was only his childishness," she said, referring to the boy.

As the old woman was about to hoist her sack on her back, the lad sprang forward to her, saying, "Let me carry it for you, Grandmother. I'm going that way."

The old woman nodded her head and put the sack on the boy's back. They then went down the street together, the old woman quite forgetting to ask Martin to pay for the apple. Martin forgot as well. He stood and watched them as they went along talking to each other.

When they were out of sight Martin went back to the house. Having found his spectacles unbroken on the steps, he picked up his awl and sat down again to work. He worked a little, but soon it was too dark for him to see well enough to pass the needle through the holes in the leather. Before long, he noticed the lamplighter passing on his way to light the street lamps.

Well, it seems it's time to light up my own lamp," he thought to himself. So he trimmed his lamp, hung it up, and sat down again to work. He finished off one boot, turned it around, and examined it closely. He could see that he had done a good job with it. Then he gathered his tools together, swept up the cuttings, and put away the needles, the thread and the awls. Then, taking down the lamp, placed it on the table.

Having done this, he took the Gospels from the shelf. He intended to open them to the same place he had marked the day before with a bit of leather, but the book opened at another place. As Martin opened the Bible to that place, his dream from last night came back to his mind. No sooner had he thought of it than he seemed to hear footsteps, as though someone were moving behind him. Martin turned around, and it seemed to him as though there were people standing in the dark corner. Yet, he couldn't make out who they were. Just then, a voice whispered in his ear: "Martin, Martin, don't you know me?"

"Who is it?" muttered Martin.

"It is I," said the voice. And out of the dark corner stepped the old man, Ivan, who smiled and then vanished like a cloud.

"It is I," said the voice again. And out of the darkness stepped the woman with the baby in her arms. The woman smiled and the baby laughed, and then they too vanished.

"It is I," said the voice once more. And the old woman and the boy with the apple stepped out, and they both smiled. They too then vanished.

And Martin's soul grew joyful. He prayed, put on his spectacles, and began reading the Gospel just where it had opened. And at the top of the page he read:

> "I was hungry, and you gave me food. I was thirsty, and you gave me drink. I was a stranger, and you took me in."

And at the bottom of the page he read:

> "Inasmuch as you did it unto one of these my brethren, even these least, you did it unto me."

And Martin understood that his dream had come true, and that the Savior had really come to him that day, and he had welcomed Him.